Hawser Martingale

Mark Rowland

A Tale of the South Sea

Hawser Martingale

Mark Rowland
A Tale of the South Sea

ISBN/EAN: 9783744709934

Printed in Europe, USA, Canada, Australia, Japan

Cover: Foto ©Andreas Hilbeck / pixelio.de

More available books at **www.hansebooks.com**

MARK ROWLAND.

A TALE OF THE SEA.

By HAWSER MARTINGALE,

AUTHOR OF "TALES OF THE OCEAN," "SALT-WATER BUBBLES,"
"JACK IN THE FORECASTLE," ETC., ETC.

"He who in 'venturous barques hath been
A wanderer on the deep,
Can tell of many an awful scene,
Where storms forever sweep."
MRS. HEMANS.

LORING, Publisher,
319 WASHINGTON STREET,
BOSTON.
1867.

Stereotyped by
ROCKWELL AND ROLLINS,
122 Wash. St., Boston.

ADDRESS TO THE READER.

THE public for years have been familiar with the tales and narratives published from time to time under the name of "Hawser Martingale;" and I am proud to say they have been received with distinguished favor. Unlike many of the sea-stories of the day, they were written by a *sailor;* and any genuine web-footed son of the sea will say that whatever demerits they may possess in other respects, the pictures of salt-water life and character they represent, are faithfully portrayed.

Although the author for several years has hardly contributed his mite to the current literature of the day, his pen has not been idle. It has not been thrown overboard, nor is it altogether rusty, as may to some extent be seen by the narrative, which is now given to the public, in which he has endeavored to sketch a series of events in the life of a sailor-boy, for the edification and amusement of persons, old or young, who take an interest in nautical scenes.

Nor will he stop here. "Hawser Martingale" will

endeavor to obey the injunction of the gallant Lawrence, and "never give up the ship" while a shot is left in the locker. And the public may be interested — perhaps gratified — to learn that unless unexpected circumstances prevent, "Mark Rowland" will be followed by other works equally entertaining, and having a decided smack of salt water.

JOHN S. SLEEPER.

ROXBURY, November, 1866.

MARK ROWLAND.

CHAPTER I.

FLATTERING DREAMS.

In the little village of Glenmaple, situated about sixty miles from Boston, resided a family some twenty years ago, whose name was Rowland. Mr. Rowland had once been possessed of some property. He married an amiable woman, and "opened a store." Fortune smiled upon him, but he became addicted to intemperate habits, which always lead to idleness and unthriftiness. He failed in business, of course, was overwhelmed with debts which he had neither the means nor the inclination to pay, and became a horse-jockey, a gambler, and a vagabond. In a word, he was one of those men, not unfrequent in New England, who start on their journey through life with brilliant prospects, but before they reach the half-way house, sacrifice their own characters and the happiness and comfort of their families to gratify a morbid thirst for intoxicating drinks.

He died miserably a few years before the commencement of my story. His widow occupied a little cottage in a lane a short distance from the main road. It was but scantily furnished, and she labored every hour in the day to procure the means of subsistence for herself and her three children.

Her neighbors respected her, notwithstanding she was poor, for she was not only industrious, but cherished correct moral principles, and a deep sense of piety, and had exerted all a woman's influence, but in vain, to keep her husband in the paths of rectitude and honor. They furnished her with work, and sometimes made her little presents, and in this way Mrs. Rowland succeeded in providing for herself and family the necessaries, if not the luxuries, of life. Being of a cheerful disposition, humble in her wishes, with her heart bound up in her children, she was grateful to divine Providence for the blessings she enjoyed, without making herself unhappy by pining after treasures which were beyond her reach.

The name of her eldest son was Mark. He was a lad of an excellent disposition and industrious habits, and was never happier than when assisting in the labors of his mother or promoting the happiness of his brother and sister. Mark was a frank, open-hearted boy, and seldom thought of self when the comfort of others was at stake. His mother had early awakened in him a thirst for knowledge, had taught him to read and write, and to value, as an inestimable treasure, the instruction he received at the district school.

Mark had for two seasons, by the labor of his hands, cultivated a little patch of ground attached to the cottage, and furnished the family with vegetables in abundance, and often placed in his mother's hands a few cents, and sometimes a piece of silver coin, which he had earned by going an errand, or performing some other service for a neighbor. He was a handy little fellow, shrewd and ingenious, as is often the case with Yankee boys.

When Mark reached the age of fourteen he was strong

and active, and remarkably intelligent, for he had read every book he could borrow, and for two years had been at the head of his school. He was also fond of athletic exercises, had climbed many a lofty pine to destroy a crow's nest, could. swim like an otter, and skate, jump, run, or wrestle with any boy of his years, and carry off the victor's wreath. In a hunt or a tramp in the woods, or at any kind of work on a farm, he could bear almost any amount of fatigue.

About this time Mark formed an intimacy with Andrew Herman, a boy a year or two older than himself, who had made two voyages to the West Indies, and was looked upon with admiration and envy by his old school-fellows in Glenmaple. After Andrew left the village to look for another voyage, Mark became silent and thoughtful. His spirits lost their wonted buoyancy. He evidently labored under the weight of some unusual care or trouble. One day his mother, who saw with anxiety this change in her son's conduct and appearance, spoke to him on the subject, and urged him to tell her the cause of the dejection which was so plainly visible in his actions and features.

"Why, mother," said Mark, "I have been thinking for some time that I am a great boy, almost able to do a man's work. Fourteen years old! Think of that, mother! I ought to do something more for the support of all of us than to remain about home, digging in the garden, loafing, or running on errands for the neighbors. Albert is old enough and strong enough to help you in the garden and in the house, and sister Ellen is no trouble to you now, and is growing older and stronger every day."

"Well, what do you think of doing, my son?"

"Mother, I am almost afraid to tell you. I should like to go to sea."

"Go to sea, Mark?" exclaimed Mrs. Rowland, greatly astonished and alarmed. "Go to sea! You cannot be serious, my son.   What could have led you to think of such a thing?"

"Why, mother, I have thought over the matter a great deal lately, and I always had a secret longing to go to sea. I have had several interesting talks with Andrew Herman. He has told me all about a sailor's life, and says I should make a capital sailor."

"I wish," said Mrs. Rowland, "that Andrew Herman had stayed on board his ship in the West Indies or any other foreign port, instead of coming back here and disturbing our quiet home by filling your head with foolish notions about a sailor's life, and longings which can never be realized."

"Why not, mother?" rejoined Mark. "I can undertake nothing that promises so well. If I go to sea I shall get good wages, for I am strong and willing to work, and bring home something every year, perhaps oftener, to furnish you and Albert and Ellen, not only with abundance of food and clothing, but other comforts, and to some extent relieve your cares, and make you all more happy! Oh, mother, *do* let me go to sea!"

"My dear child," said Mrs. Rowland, and the tears came into her eyes, "a sailor's life is full of hardship, danger, and fatigue; and what if you should be shipwrecked, or cast away on some desert shore, or fall overboard and be drowned, or be captured by pirates, or die of some terrible disease in a foreign land, and no mother to nurse you or comfort you in your dying hour! Oh, Mark, I can never consent to your going to sea."

"Mother, Andrew Herman says that such objections to a sailor's life are all humbugs. He says, and surely he ought to know, that in a good ship there is no danger of being cast away or shipwrecked. He says a sailor's life is a jolly one, free from care, with nothing to do but watch the sails and trim them, while the pleasant breezes waft you bravely over the seas. Besides, according to his account, the sailors are such jovial companions, all the time laughing and frolicking, or telling stories or singing songs; and then, the wonders to be seen on the waters and in foreign lands! and the wild and romantic adventures in store!"

"My son," replied the widow Rowland, "Andrew Herman has not given you a true description of a sailor's life. I know it is beset with toils and difficulties and dangers innumerable."

"Mother, I have often heard you say that God watches over us wherever we may be, and that the widow and the orphan are his especial care; and surely his kind influence will be felt as much on the ocean as on the land."

"That is true, my son; we are never beyond his protecting power. Nevertheless, Mark, I feel as if I cannot part with you for such a purpose. The mere idea of such a project makes me sick at heart. But, enough now. We will talk of this at some other time. In the mean while we may perhaps think of some employment for you, of a different nature, which will prevent any necessity for your going abroad and exposing yourself to the perils and hardships of a sailor's life, and they are many, I know, notwithstanding the bewitching pictures so vividly sketched by Andrew Herman."

Some weeks passed away, and nothing occurred to change the current of Mark Rowland's feelings. He could find no employment of a satisfactory character in the vicinity of his home. He was offered by Mr. Sanson the situation of clerk and errand-boy in his grocery store, with wages little more than nominal. But Mr. Sanson's store was the resort at times of loafers, vagabonds, and drunkards, for he sold strong liquors by the glass. Indeed, he boasted that this disgraceful branch of his business was the source of his greatest profit. But Mrs. Rowland recollected her husband's failings.

She had suffered, deeply suffered, from the evils of intemperance, and loathed the very sight or name of a "dramshop." She would sooner have seen Mark in his grave than stooping to such degrading work, even if he had been offered wages enough to supply all her wants.

Mark could easily have procured employment as a farmer's boy; but all that he would receive for his labor, certainly for one or two years, would be his maintenance and clothing. The result would be the same if he became an apprentice to a blacksmith or a joiner. He was anxious to be earning something immediately, for he knew that his mother, although she never was heard to repine at her lot, was compelled by poverty to deny herself many things which would greatly contribute to the comfort of herself and family.

Mrs. Rowland pondered often and deeply on the subject which Mark had broached. She felt it would be difficult to shake his inclination to go to sea. She knew that the sooner her son was engaged in any regular business the better it would be for him and for all of them. He was tall and robust, and more manly in his character as well as form than one would suppose from his years. His principles were good, and seemed firmly rooted. She was convinced that he possessed firmness and strength of mind to resist temptations to evil, and triumph over all bad influences. If he went to sea, and proved fortunate in his undertakings, he might by his intelligence, enterprise, and energy rise rapidly in his profession, and in a few years become an officer, and ultimately master of a ship, and have it in his power to frighten away the ills of poverty which seemed to cling closer to her every year, and help his brother and sister if she should be called away to another and a better world.

After a severe struggle with her feelings, and frequent discussions with Mark, who urged his point with great earnestness, Mrs. Rowland gave her reluctant consent that her son should go to Boston, and try to find an opportunity to go to sea as a cabin-boy. She put his few plain and homely clothes in the best possible order ; she talked to him long and often in relation to his conduct while away from home, and sought to fortify his mind against allurements and tendencies to evil.

At length the morning arrived when Mark was to depart for the great metropolis of New England, as a starting-point from which to make his way in the world. He knew no one in that busy place on whom he could call for advice or assistance. He had no letters of introduction to business-men. But he had confidence in himself, and looked boldly into the future without misgivings. It was a sad day for the poor widow. She made up a small bundle for her son, consisting of articles of clothing, and a slender stock of necessaries, not forgetting a Bible. She placed in his hands a little money which she had contrived to save from her hard earnings, and while the tears ran down her cheeks she took him in her arms, bade God bless him, and Mark sat out on his journey.

He travelled along slowly at first, with his bundle slung on a stick, which rested on his shoulder. He was sorry to see the anguish of his mother, and even doubted whether he had acted right in thus wringing from her a slow consent to encounter the dangers of the seas. He was strongly tempted to return and tell his mother that he would abandon all idea of seeking to improve his fortunes abroad, but would remain with her and do what he could to make her happy. And then again he would view the subject in a different light. He felt assured that his mother would soon recover from the dejected state in which he had left her, for he well knew her fortitude and her trust in an overruling Providence.

Mark was always of an adventurous disposition, and from the time when he first read " Robinson Crusoe," which one of his school-fellows loaned him, he had cherished a longing for a roving life. That book has doubtless caused many noble, daring spirits to leave the comforts of home and the enjoyments of domestic life to seek for wild adventures and romantic incidents abroad. Besides, Mark did not anticipate any misfortunes. He looked, as youths are apt to look, on the sunny side of life, without seeing the storms and tornadoes which are gathering in the distance. He figured to himself the delight of his mother when he should return from a voyage to a foreign land stout, hearty, and cheerful, and fling into her lap a pile of Spanish dollars. As he indulged in thoughts like these his step was quicker and more vigorous, and his features lost the pensive expression which had been occasioned by parting with those he loved, and kindled with excitement and joy.

He travelled onward, hardly stopping to rest until the sun had sank behind a wood-crowned height, around whose base he had winded his way, and on inquiring he found, to his great satisfaction, that he had accomplished fully one third of his journey. He sat down on a rock by the wayside, and took from his bundle some provisions which his mother had provided him with, and made a frugal meal, after which he satisfied his thirst from a brook which ran murmuring along at the side of the road, and proceeded on his journey. As the shades of evening fell, however, he became decidedly tired, and acknowledged to himself that some repose to his wearied limbs would be exceedingly grateful. He had now reached the snug-looking dwelling-house of a thrifty farmer in the town of Westville, and finding Mr. Drummond, the owner of the establishment, standing near the gate of the barn-yard talking with a neighbor, Mark respectfully asked permission to sleep in the barn on the hay-mow for the night.

The kind-hearted farmer was somewhat astonished at the

request; he looked hard at Mark, and instead of replying, asked him a few questions, which were so satisfactorily answered, that he insisted on our young adventurer going with him to the house, where he was introduced to the farmer's wife, a cheerful, motherly-looking woman, who set before him a capacious bowl of bread and milk, and a mammoth slice of newly-made cheese; and afterwards led him to a chamber in which he found an excellent bed, where he soon fell asleep, and continued in that state until awakened by the sun shining into his chamber on the following morning.

Mark Rowland was no sluggard, and he felt mortified at having slept so long. He soon dressed himself and went below, where he was kindly greeted, and found an excellent breakfast already prepared, of which he was urged, by his hospitable entertainers, to partake, in language so kind that he could not refuse. After breakfast he thanked Mr. Drummond and his wife for their hospitality, and throwing his bundle over his shoulder, proceeded on his journey towards Boston. He looked upon this happy incident, finding kind and sympathizing friends among utter strangers, as a good augury, and his heart grew lighter as he passed along. He hummed an old song, which his mother had often sung; he whistled, but not for want of thought.

It was towards noon on the third day of his journey that, from one of the hills in the neighborhood of Boston, he first beheld the great metropolis. He stopped a few minutes, and gazed admiringly on the grand city, with its towers and spires reaching far upwards from immense masses of brick, with the broad dome of the State House surmounting the whole. He then hurried along, overjoyed at having so nearly reached the termination of his journey. He passed over Charlestown bridge, and soon found himself in the midst of the great and populous city. Mark Rowland inquired the

2

way to the wharves, for it was there he expected to find a ship in which to make his first voyage to sea. But how he was to get a situation, whom he was to address, or in what manner he should make application for employment, he had not the slightest idea. His notions of seafaring matters were, of course, very vague, yet he had a tongue in his head, and knew how to use it, and did not for a moment doubt of ultimate success. But if fortune had not greatly favored him, he might have waited long and been subjected to much inconvenience before he could have accomplished his object.

As he passed along through the city, Mark was almost stupefied at the sight of the many strange and beautiful objects around him. The multitude of houses, the elegance of the stores and their contents, the beauty and vastness of the public buildings, the numerous vehicles rattling over the pavements, the throngs of people threading the narrow streets in every direction, all attracted his attention, and almost bewildered him. After passing through numerous streets, and making many inquiries, he found himself on one of the principal wharves, which was lined with ships, brigs, and schooners, taking in or discharging cargoes of merchandise, while apparently great bustle and confusion reigned on their decks.

Mark had never seen a ship, but he had often looked at pictures of them under full sail with a deep interest. He now stood by the side of a real ship, on Long Wharf, and gazed upon it with admiration. He examined it with eagerness from stem to stern, from the truck to the deck, and wondered at its huge bulk, its massive spars, and the countless variety of ropes which, crossing each other, extended in every direction. He proceeded further down the wharf, and looked beyond the ships, and saw the waters of Boston Bay, and vessels sailing, and boats moving gracefully along, with ensigns and pennants waving at the mast-head. That was a happy moment. It seemed to Mark Rowland that he stood in fairy-land, and that the romantic dreams which had often visited him in his sleep at length were realized.

CHAPTER II.

MARK ROWLAND stood on the wharf, gazing for a long time, on the busy and attractive scenes around him. At length he thought of the object of his visit to the city; and, after examining the features of various persons who were standing around, or engaged in some employment, he approached a gentleman whose benevolent countenance won his confidence, and accosting him in a respectful manner, asked him if he knew of a captain who wanted a cabin-boy.

The gentleman whom he addressed was a wealthy merchant, and at that time was busily employed in fitting a ship away for the East Indies. He looked at Mark, and was pleased with the frank and manly expression of his features, his modest manner, and general appearance. He took a liking to the lad at once, so true it is that goodness, or even the semblance of goodness, will always meet with friends. He inquired of the young stranger his name, his residence, the condition of his parents, and how it happened that he came such a distance, alone and on foot, without money or friends, to the city, in search of a voyage to sea. To these questions Mark answered promptly and satisfactorily, and the merchant was convinced that he spoke the truth, and was deserving of encouragement and assistance.

Mr. Fortesque, that was the name of the merchant, told our young adventurer that he had a large ship called the

Saladin, which was to sail in a few days for Calcutta in the East Indies; that the ship would be commanded by a very worthy man, and that Mark should have the situation of cabin-boy. One can hardly conceive the joy of Mark when he heard the words of the benevolent merchant. His good fortune, in thus so easily obtaining a voyage to sea, equalled his most sanguine expectations, and, with words of deep feeling, he thanked Mr. Fortesque again and again.

Mr. Fortesque took Mark immediately on board the ship, and introduced him to the captain, whose name was Somers, as cabin-boy of the Saladin. It was soon arranged that, as Mark was a stranger in Boston, and had no boarding-house or friends, or means of procuring food and lodging, he should remain on board the ship, there partake of his meals, and sleep in the cabin. He was pleased with this arrangement, and lost no time in learning his duties and making himself useful in every possible way. Before the ship left the wharf he succeeded in gaining the good-will of the captain and the mates, as well as the owner; for he showed himself willing, obedient, active, and intelligent.

The sailors to compose the crew were soon shipped, and Mark's wages were fixed at eight dollars a month. Mr. Fortesque generously supplied him with some necessary clothing, and he was thus enabled to send back to his mother, not only all the money she had given him, but five dollars out of his two months' advance pay. He inclosed it in a letter, in which he exultingly described his good fortune and happy feelings, spoke in grateful terms of the kindness of Mr. Fortesque, and assured his mother that, in a year at farthest, he should return to Boston with a purse well filled, the result of his own exertions, and hasten home on the wings of affection.

On the following day the wind was fair, the weather was pleasant, the crew were mustered, the pilot came on board,

2*

the top-sails were loosed and hoisted up, the fasts cast off, and, with a fair wind and ebb tide, the Saladin proceeded gallantly down the harbor, and was soon outside of Boston light-house, on her way to the distant East Indies. Mark took a long look at the land, as it lessened in the distance, and mentally bade adieu to the loved ones he left behind him.

The Saladin proved to be a strong, safe, and comfortable ship, but was rather a dull sailer, and moved along heavily through the water. Captain Somers was a noble-hearted man, who understood his business thoroughly. He treated Mark with kindness, and protected him during the early part of the passage from the rude conduct and rough practical jokes of the sailors. But it was not long before the good qualities of the cabin-boy became known and acknowledged, and he acquired rapidly some knowledge of a seafaring life, and was so cheerful, so obliging, so industrious, so active, and so intelligent, that he made a friend of every man on board. He was a favorite with all, and so far from being the subject of ill-natured gibes or jokes, he was treated with kindness and indulgence, not only by the officers, but by every sailor in the ship.

Mark was rather pleased with a sailor's life, — it was a mode of life which suited his bold, adventurous disposition, — but the true wish of his heart was to gain knowledge, that kind of knowledge which can only be derived from study, from books, and prepare him for taking a high stand for usefulness among his fellow-men. Nevertheless, he bade fair to make a good sailor. So said Captain Somers, and so said his officers. It was plain that Mark Rowland would make friends, in whatever path of life he might choose to tread — and such will always be the case. A youth, if he possesses honesty, industry, a cheerful temper, and cherishes a desire to do right, and contribute to the happiness of others, will always meet with encouragement and aid from the good and deserving part of mankind.

The Saladin proceeded merrily on her voyage, and new wonders were witnessed by Mark every day — the wonders of the ocean, which those who dwell peaceably and quietly on the land can hardly imagine. The cheerful influence of a fine breeze, when the vessel dashes gloriously forward on her way; the long swell and smooth surface of the sea in a calm; the flashing phosphorescence of the sea-water during the night; the strict order and discipline on board a well-regulated ship; the activity of the sailors as they made or took in sail, and their encouraging shouts, or songs, marking time, as they pulled heavily at the ropes; the flights of sea-birds, the spouting of whales, and the gambols of those queer-looking fish known as porpoises, all attracted his attention and excited his wonder. Indeed, every succeeding day showed him something new and remarkable. And the Saladin had not been many days on her voyage before an opportunity was given for Mark Rowland to witness the rise, progress, and ordinary effects of a gale of wind at sea.

The gale came on gradually, after a steady and increasing breeze from the northward for a couple of days. The light sails, as the flying-jib and royals and studding-sails, were first taken in — then the top-gallant sails and jib. The wind increased as darkness came on; the heavens became obscured with thick, flying clouds, and all hands were called to reef top-sails. This operation, under the judicious management of the captain, who superintended the work, was executed with adroitness and dispatch, and two reefs were taken in the fore and mizzen top-sails, and one in the main, and the royal-yards were sent down on deck. The gale continued to increase, and the wind hauled to the eastward. It began to rain, with every prospect, in the language of Mr. Smeaton, the second mate, of "a greasy night."

At midnight, the watch below, as well as the cook, steward, and cabin-boy, were told to hurry up on deck, to take in more sail. The main-sail was clued up and handed, a couple of reefs taken in the spanker, and the top-sails were close-reefed. The sea was now much agitated. The waves followed each other in swift succession, and the spray in dense volumes broke over the bows and sometimes deluged the waist, as the ship plunged along through the water. Mark Rowland, while lending a hand to haul out the weather foretop-sail reef-tackle, got his first thorough ducking in salt water, to the great amusement of the sailors.

By two o'clock in the morning Captain Somers found it expedient to "lay the ship to" under a close-reefed main-top-sail. Every other sail was now taken in, and snugly furled, and the top-gallant yards were sent down and the top-gallant masts housed. The helm was put in one position, "hard-a-lee," and firmly lashed. The Saladin was found to lay to under this sail remarkably well; the waves, as they rushed madly along, threatening to overwhelm the decks, passed beneath the ship, as she courteously rose to meet them, or expended their force on the weather-bow, sending cataracts of spray over the decks.

The ship now, while lying to, made very little head-way, but was driven to leeward by the mighty power of the wind and the waves, forced bodily through the water at the rate of two or three knots, and making some five or six points leeway. Thus, while by compass the head of the ship pointed towards east-southeast, the course actually made was nearly south. It is this unavoidable leeway in a gale, when a ship cannot carry sail, that makes the sailors so much rejoice in "plenty of sea room," and dread the dangers of a lee-shore.

For twelve hours the Saladin lay to, until the wind exhausted itself, after giving two or three extra puffs, as if determined to capsize the ship, or blow the masts away.

Mark Rowland was at first not a little startled at the strange and wild phenomena and varied incidents which attend a gale of wind at sea. It would be difficult to say whether they most excited his fear or his admiration. At such a time the hoarse whistling and singing of the wind through the rigging, the crashing noise of the breaking billows as they came rushing onward with a wild roar, and passed harmlessly by, the incessant creaking and groaning of the bulkheads and timbers, the continual tossing about, rolling and pitching, and convulsive jerking of the ship, which seemed at such a moment an object utterly insignificant, a mere plaything, a toy, to furnish sport for the elements, all constitute a scene which for sublimity probably has no parallel. Indeed, a severe gale of wind in a stout ship, well manned, and so skilfully managed as to preclude the idea of imminent peril, is one of the most interesting and exciting events which can be met with in life. It is worth almost any sacrifice on the part of a landsman to witness and enjoy.

Mark's apprehension of danger, which such a novel and sublime scene would naturally excite, were greatly lessened by noting the calm and cheerful manner of the captain and his officers, who attended to their various duties as self-possessed and fearless as if they could control the action of the elements.

A few days after the Saladin had been visited by this tempest, and about twenty days after leaving port, one beautiful morning just as the sun was rising above the horizon, and while the good ship was sailing along with a light but favorable breeze over a smooth sea at the rate of some three or four knots, Mark Rowland, who was standing opposite the galley, looking over the bulwarks to leeward, his thoughts far away, was hailed by Mr. Jarls, the first officer, whose watch was on deck at the time, and ordered to go aloft, take a look around the horizon, and see if any vessels were in sight. Mark sprang into the rigging with alacrity, and in a marvellous short time was on the fore-top-gallant yard, scanning with a pair of sharp eyes the distant horizon.

He had been in this position but a few minutes when he called to the mate at the top of his voice, " Mr. Jarls! Mr. Jarls! "

" Hallo! " replied that vigilant officer; " what's in the wind now? "

" I see something on the water," said Mark. " 'Tis not a ship, for it has no sails. It is far away, in that direction," continued Mark, pointing across the weather-bow.

" What does it look like? " asked the mate.

" It looks like a vessel partly sunk, with two short masts sticking out of the water," replied the boy.

" Perhaps it is Old Neptune himself," said Mr. Jarls, quietly, " taking an airing by steam! But we are not far enough along for him yet. He will undoubtedly be on board in good time." So saying the mate bounded into the fore rigging, and in a few seconds was on the fore-top-sail yard. He looked intently in the direction indicated by Mark, and then in his loudest tone shouted, "WRECK, HO! " Captain Somers, roused out of his sleep by the rough voice of the mate hailing the fore-top-gallant yard, by this time was on deck. He immediately ordered the studding-sails to be taken in, the yards braced up, and the ship steered in the direction of the wreck.

A wreck at sea is a solemn sight. Every true sailor feels deep sympathy for others in distress, and will labor with might and main to render assistance. He knows not how soon he may be in the same unfortunate plight himself. It was soon ascertained that the wreck was that of a ship with her masts broken off, and evidently full of water. As the Saladin drew towards the wreck something like a flag was seen flying a few feet above the galley, or caboose-house.

"There are some living souls on board that hulk!" exclaimed Captain Somers, with unusual energy, "and we must rescue them from their terrible situation, at all hazards. Clear away the quarter-boat, Mr. Smeaton!" said he to the second mate; "get ready to start for the wreck as soon as we lay the maintop-sail to the mast."

And now the object which excited so much interest could be plainly seen from the waist. The sea was comparatively smooth, nevertheless the waves washed across the deck from plankshear to plankshear, giving little hope of finding any living person attached to this still floating wreck. The galley seemed split and shattered, but the doors were apparently closed. Nothing bearing the resemblance of a human being was seen about the decks, nor were there any signs of life. But the tattered garment fastened to a small spar, and displayed from the top of the caboose-house, was proof enough that some one, perhaps more than one of that ship's company had survived, for a time at least, the terrible disaster. Were any living persons now on board? If so, how wretched must be their fate! That galley! what did the signal on its summit portend?

The Saladin continued her course until almost within hail of the sunken vessel, when her way was suddenly stopped by putting the helm hard down, and laying the maintop-sail aback. The quarter-boat was now lowered, and Mr. Smeaton, with a stout boat's crew, pushed off to board the wreck. On going alongside, no living being was visible; no one came forth from that galley. The second mate hailed and shouted with a voice loud enough to have awakened the

Seven Sleepers, but there was no reply. He hailed again and again, with the same result.

"There is no one here!" he exclaimed, turning round to the boat's crew, "we may as well go back to the ship."

"I'll take a look into that galley first, sir, if you have no objection," said Jack Manwell, a whole-hearted young sailor belonging to Marblehead. "There's no knowing what sort of treasures we may find there!"

The officer nodded assent, — he could not well refuse, — and Jack jumped on the main deck of the ill-fated vessel. He tried to open the nearest door of the caboose-house, but found the operation a difficult one; the door seemed jammed, or fastened on the inside. An oar was passed him from the boat, by the aid of which he succeeded in forcing open the door, when a sad spectacle was presented to his view.

A man, pale, haggard, with fixed, staring eyes, preternaturally large, and an expression of intolerable anguish, which was truly appalling to look upon, was seated on the platform of the caboose, his head leaning against the side of the galley. Across his knees, and encircled in his arms, was the body of a woman, with her head hanging down and apparently lifeless. Both were almost destitute of clothing. One seemed to be already dead, and the other dying of cold and hunger!

"Hallo, shipmates!" said Jack Manwell, in a cheerful voice, "you have a snug berth of it here, all to yourselves. Come, rouse and bitt! There are better lodgings hard by, with pea-jackets and plenty of grub; for you seem to have been on short allowance of everything but salt water."

The man made no attempt to rise from his recumbent position. He stared for a moment vacantly at the sailor, then dropped his eyes to the wilted body that he held in his arms, and faintly murmured, "My wife, my wife!"

"Oh, never mind your wife," said Jack, gently disengaging the woman from the arms of her husband. "She will do well enough yet; when we get her on board the Saladin, we will bring her to with a 'yeo heave O,' and a double-shuffle to come up with."

By this time Mr. Smeaton and one of the seamen were at the door of the galley. The woman was not dead. She had fainted from exhaustion; but her pulse still beat, and she exhibited other signs of life. With much difficulty she was placed in the boat. Then the man, who was unable to walk, or even stand without support, was assisted across the deck, and placed by the side of his wife. The boat was then shoved off, and in a few minutes was alongside of the Saladin, to leeward.

These two unfortunate beings, with the utmost care and tenderness, were taken on board the ship, the rough-looking sailors manifesting the most heart-felt sympathy for their wretched condition. They were carried into the cabin; warmth was imparted to their limbs, and gentle restoratives applied. For some days their souls seemed to be hovering on the verge of eternity, but by careful nursing and a course of judicious treatment on the part of Captain Somers, they both revived, gradually recovered strength, and were finally restored to health. More than a week passed, however, before either of them felt able to communicate the details of the terrible disaster, of which they had been the victims.

The vessel which the sharp eyes of Mark Rowland discovered in a foundered condition was the ship Clarion, of Salem, bound on a voyage to Maranham, in Brazil, having a quantity of lumber in the hold, and her "between decks" filled with an assortment of miscellaneous articles. In this ship Mr. James S. Rivington, a merchant who had been for several years engaged in trade with the north coast of Brazil, had taken passage, accompanied by his wife. These two persons were the only passengers.

3

The Clarion experienced the severe gale of wind, which the Saladin weathered without the slightest injury. During the gale the captain of the Clarion assured Mr. and Mrs. Rivington that there was no cause for fear. The ship was strongly built, in good condition, and an excellent sea-boat. In the middle of the Atlantic, with plenty of sea-room, they were as safe with such a mere capful of wind, as if standing on Boston Common on a summer's day, gazing at "the big elm." This assurance, and the confident aspect of the sailors, as they attended to their duties, in a great measure relieved the minds of the passengers from a load of anxiety.

The gale continued through the day and the following night. Towards morning Mr. Rivington heard the first officer enter the cabin and tell the captain that there was a dangerous sea running, and the ship lay-to badly, often falling off into the trough of the sea. The captain hastened on deck, and soon afterwards the second mate, who had the watch below, was roused out to lend a hand to get the ship off the wind to scud before the gale.

Mr. Rivington now, with his state-room door wide open, eagerly listened for sounds on deck to indicate what was going on. In less than five minutes he heard the captain give the orders, "Hoist the foretop-mast stay-sail! hard up your helm! square away the after-yards!" A great trampling was then heard overhead, which was soon succeeded by a thundering shock, and it seemed as if the cataract of Niagara had been poured on the quarter-deck. The ship was hurled over with giant force, nearly on her beam-ends; every timber seemed wrenched from its place, the affrighted passengers were thrown out of their berths against the bulkhead, badly bruised and nearly stunned, and the cabin was half-filled with water!

As soon as the ship righted, and the overwhelming wave, having done its work of destruction, quietly rolled away,

Mr. Rivington and his wife, confused, terrified, convinced
that some dreadful catastrophe had occurred, waded through
the water, waist deep, to the companion-way, and groped
their way to the deck, as to a place of comparative safety.

A gloomy spectacle awaited them there. The sea was
making a fair breach over the decks, but not a human being
was to be seen. The wind screeched, and the broken spars
thumped against the sides of the ship, but not the faintest
sound of a human voice reached their ears!

Mr. Rivington, horror-stricken at this sudden disaster,
shouted for the captain, for the mates, for some living being,
but received no answer. Clinging to the bulwarks, and at
the imminent risk of his life, he went forward, put his head
down the fore-scuttle and hailed the crew, but the only response from the forecastle was the plash of the water against
the bowsprit bitts, as it washed backward and forward!

Darkness and the dense atmosphere caused by a mingling
of the rain and the spoondrift, added to the horrors of the
scene. The wind seemed at times to lull, and Mr. Rivington looked anxiously around for a glimmering of daylight.
He could not conceal from himself the awful fact that the
ship was gradually sinking, and that all hands, officers and
sailors, all, had been swept overboard while engaged in the
attempt to get the ship before the wind! All had been
called without a moment's warning, to appear before the
judgment seat of God!

The fate of the two passengers seemed even more terrible
than that of the crew. Their misery was prolonged, with
the prospect of death in his most hideous shape not far off.
They were exposed without shelter or clothing on the deck
of the sinking vessel to the whole fury of the tempest, with
sheets of salt water drenching them every moment. Mr.
Rivington lashed his wife and himself to the fife-rail, near

the mizzen-mast, and in this wretched condition they awaited the abatement of the gale and the light of day.

Daylight came at last, but brought no comfort. Although the wind had diminished, and the waves had partially subsided, daylight only showed the unhappy couple more distinctly their forlorn and hopeless condition. The ship's deck amidships was now nearly on a level with the ocean. The mizzen-mast, by the weight of the sea which came on board, was broken off about six feet from the deck; the main-mast was broken off just below the top, and, in falling over the side, carried the foretop-mast along with it. The ship's boats, spars, barrels, lumber, and movable things of every description, were washed overboard by the destructive wave. The caboose-house or galley, a mere box, encasing the cooking-stove or caboose, situated well forward, and strongly lashed to ringbolts in the deck, was left standing, but was shaken and shattered by the angry billows. These facts showed beyond doubt that while all hands were aft bracing round the yards, the ship had been struck by a combing sea, which came in over the quarter, and spent all its force on the after part of the vessel and the waist.

The buoyant nature of the cargo prevented the ship from sinking, although full of water. Mr. and Mrs. Rivington took possession of the galley, as a place of refuge, but their situation was pitiable in the extreme. Without clothing to protect them from the weather, without provisions of any kind, and also destitute of water, in the midst of the wide ocean, with no prospect of being seen and rescued by any passing vessel, during the few days of intense suffering before death would come to their relief, they might well give themselves up to despair!

Mr. Rivington found in the galley a piece of an old garment belonging to the cook, which he managed to hoist, with but faint hope that it would be seen by any friendly bark,

and contribute to their deliverance. Four days this unfortunate couple passed in this dreadful condition, and many
and fervent were their prayers to the Almighty for succor in
the hour of need. The gnawings of hunger and thirst drove
them almost to madness. Their strength gradually departed.
Their courage failed them, and even the faint glimmerings
of hope faded away. But at the last moment, when death
had already marked them for his prey, the ship Saladin came
sailing along, the sharp eyes of Mark Rowland saw the
wreck afar off, and the husband and wife were taken from
the wreck, and relieved from sufferings too acute and soul-
rending for imagination to conceive.

3*

CHAPTER III.

On the night after Mr. Rivington had told the story of the disaster with its thrilling details, Mark Rowland stayed late on deck in the first watch, and listened to the conversation among the sailors, who, seated cosily on the heel of the bowsprit or the windlass end, freely discussed subjects connected with the wreck.

" 'Tis a great pity," said a rough-looking old tar, named Nicholas Haxon, who had passed a large portion of his life on the salt water, but who still cherished a sailor's characteristic devotion for the gentler sex; " 'tis a great pity that the poor woman had no one with her in her trouble but her husband, a fresh-water chap, who, I'll bet a biscuit, can't tell the difference between a marline-spike and a handspike, and is as green as the backbone of a gar-fish. If a real sailor had been on board and steered clear of the clutches of Davy Jones, he would have fished up something to wear and something to eat, and would have contrived a better lodging-place than that old galley."

"Avast there!" exclaimed Ned Thrumbo, one of his watch-mates; " clap a stopper on your jaw rope, if it veers out such stuff as that. The ship was swamped, and her decks were cleared of everything but the galley. Nothing could be fished from the steerage or the cabin without a diving-bell or a grapnell. The man did the best for his wife and himself that could be done. He deserves credit rather than blame for comforting the poor woman, holding her in his arms to warm her chilled frame, and keeping her alive as long as he did. All the web-footed gentry in the world, had they been on board, could not have mended the matter, and whoever says otherwise is a fool and a know-nothing. Poor little soul! She has had misery enough during the last week to make her despise salt water for the rest of her life."

"She is doing well now, and so is her husband, according to the captain's account," said Jack Manwell. "It was a lucky thing that we fell in with the wreck as we did. A few hours more would have brought them both up with a round turn. That was a bright thought of Mr. Jarls, to send the cabin-boy aloft at sunrise to take a look around the horizon."

"It was so!" exclaimed Ned Thrumbo, with energy. "If I had the power, I would compel every skipper that crosses the ocean to see that a good lookout is kept from aloft every hour in the day. In bad weather there should be a crow's-nest in the cross-trees, after the fashion of the whalers. We know not how many lives might be saved by steering such a course."

"Cases have been known," said Nicholas Haxon, "where poor sailors clinging to a raft or a wreck, have been passed quite near, almost within hail, without being seen, and were afterwards picked up by some vessel that kept a better lookout."

"That's true," said Jack, "and I often go aloft and take a careful look round, half expecting to see some brother sailor on a floating spar, or clinging to a life-buoy. Some captains, however, care not a ropeyarn for such things, so long as they make quick and safe passages. Aye, and some there are who would not go a point out of their way to take a poor fellow off a wreck, if they fell in with one."

"Hallo!" said Ned Thrumbo, ever disposed to look on

the bright side, "you have lost your reckoning, Jack! No sailor would refuse to lend a helping hand to a shipmate in distress. If such a fellow could be found, and I had my way, he should be fed for six months on a short allowance of gulf-weed and bilge-water, and touched up with a rope's end every hour while he lives on such diet."

"And serve him right, too!" said Jack Manwell. "But, as Nicholas says, such cases *have* occurred; some such hardened scoundrels have sailed the ocean; but I may say for the credit of human nature in general, and salt-water life in particular, are very seldom met with, and when met with, should have the mark of a Cain stamped on their foreheads, that they may be known on sea or on land."

"I have heard of such monsters, but never -believed in them," said Ned; "I always looked upon such stories as a slander on the whole web-footed tribe. Did you ever *know* a case, Jack, where a crew was left to perish in a sinking ship, by an unfeeling ship-master?"

"Yes," promptly replied Jack Manwell; "it happened before I was born, in the year 1807. I have heard my mother tell all about it thousands of times, and she was one of the principal actors in the play. At the time, it was much talked of all over the country, and many years will pass away before it is forgotten in Marblehead, where, I am sorry to say, the monster lived."

"What was his name?" asked Ned.

"His name was Floyd Ireson, and he was skipper of a fishing schooner. Returning one fall from the Banks, and when only a few hours' sail from port, he fell in with a wreck, on which were three or four helpless creatures clinging to the rigging, and dying by inches. The heartless skipper would not go to their assistance, and when remonstrated with by one of his men, he clinched his refusal wit.

a disgusting oath, and kept on the course towards his home."

"And was there not heart and manliness enough among the crew," asked Ned Thrumbo, "to wrest the vessel out of the hands of the skipper, and steer a straight course for the sinking wreck?"

"That would never do," said Nicholas Haxon. "Such doings would be mutiny, and the whole crew would be imprisoned for life, or strung up by the gills like a parcel of stock-fish. Obey orders if you break owners, is my doctrine, and a safe one."

"But not mine when the lives of fellow-creatures are at stake," rejoined the warm-hearted Ned Thrumbo; "and I don't believe a jury, even of landsmen, would hang a man or send him to the State prison for doing what everybody knows is right in the eyes of God and man."

"The cowardly fellows in the fishing schooner did not steer according to your chart, Ned," said Jack Manwell, resuming the thread of his narrative. "They condemned the cruel conduct of the skipper, but had not courage to put the stony-hearted scoundrel in irons, take possession of the schooner, and take off those unfortunate men from the wreck. The vessel in a few hours arrived in the harbor of Marblehead, and the men hastened ashore and created a great commotion among the people by exposing the conduct of the skipper. A vessel was immediately despatched to look for the wreck and rescue any of the poor fellows who might be living. But it was too late; the wreck was never found, and the unfortunate men who were seen lashed to the rigging, and raising their hands, imploring assistance, without doubt miserably perished."

"And what became of the skipper?" inquired Ned Thrumbo. "Was there no law to bring him to his bearings, and give him a taste of the cat-o'-nine-tails? I should like to have been the boatswain's mate to lay it on."

"No law could reach him for such an act," said Jack. "But the people—old and young, men, women, and children—collected together, and resolved to punish him. At first, they determined to lynch him by hanging him to a sign-post. But this plan was abandoned. Nevertheless, his house was surrounded, and he was hauled out of his hiding-place, pale and trembling, and begging for mercy. He received on the spot many kicks and cuffs from his indignant townsmen, and was then stripped to the skin and gloriously tarred and feathered, until he looked like a giant penguin. He was hoisted on a platform in a cart drawn by oxen, and carried in procession through every part of the town, amid the hootings and curses of the populace. He was severely punished for his barbarity. Some months passed before he recovered from the injuries he received, and he never went to sea afterwards in any capacity; but remained in Marble-head, where he lived for many years, universally despised. Whenever he appeared in the streets, which was not often, the boys would mock him and hallo after him, or sing in rude chorus,—

> "'There goes Floyd Ireson, who, for his hard heart,
>   Was tarred and feathered and carried in a cart
>   By the women of Marblehead.'"

"And served him right," said Ned. "'Tis a pity, though, that they had not lynched him at once, while they had a chance. Such a fellow did not deserve to live, and the laws which would not hang such a fellow are not worth a piece of old junk."

After Mr. and Mrs. Rivington had been a fortnight on board the Saladin, a ship was seen astern rapidly coming up. It proved to be the ship Primrose, of New York, bound to

Pernambuco. The Primrose was hove-to at the request of Captain Somers, who went on board and related to the master of the Primrose the distressing circumstances connected with the foundering of the Clarion, and the rescue of Mr. and Mrs. Rivington from the wreck, and also stating that it was their earnest wish to be transferred to the Primrose and landed at Pernambuco.

To this arrangement no objection was made, and the two passengers, after expressing their warmest thanks to Captain Somers, his officers and crew, for their gallant and generous conduct, and assuring Mark Rowland that they should never forget his services, but remember him with kind and grateful feelings, as it was his sharp eyes which discovered the wreck, left the Saladin, amid the loudly-expressed kind wishes and cheers of the sailors, and in a few minutes were on board the Primrose on their way to Pernambuco.

As the ship Saladin advanced into the tropical latitudes, new wonders excited the admiration of Mark Rowland. He beheld the flights of flying-fish as they gracefully skimmed along over the surface of the ocean, sometimes in sport, and sometimes to escape from the jaws of some devouring monster; he beheld the enormous masses and belts of gulf-weed which the ship passed through day after day, and week after week, in that part of the Atlantic known as the Sargossa Sea, and which serves as the habitation of myriads of shell-fish of many varieties; he saw the dolphin, — not the tunny-fish, the dolphin of the ancients, but the beautiful, swift, and graceful animal, clad in purple and gold, which sailors love to look upon and welcome on board, for they always anticipate with his coming the pleasant idea of " a glorious chowder for all hands." He saw the boneta, the albicore, and the barracooter, and on one occasion narrowly escaped being devoured by a shark!

This startling event took place one pleasant afternoon,

when some sixty or eighty miles to the westward of the Cape de Verde Islands. The easterly breeze which had been gradually lessening for some days had almost died away, and the ship had hardly steerage way, moving through the water at the rate of only one or one and a half knots. A goodly supply of fowls had been put on board in Boston, for the benefit of those who lived in the cabin, and many of them still remained in the coops. These were under the direct charge of the cabin-boy ; but Mr. Smeaton, the second officer, also took an interest in their welfare, and from a motive not altogether unselfish, inasmuch as he was very fond of fowls, especially when served up in the form of a fricassee, or curried-stew, or a chicken-pie.

About six bells, or three o'clock, while Mr. Smeaton and the watch on deck were forward attending to some necessary duty, and Mr. Jarls was writing his log in the cabin, and Captain Somers was taking a quiet nap in his state-room, one of the inmates of the coop, a stately rooster, an especial favorite, seeing no one on the quarter-deck but the helmsman, who was nodding at his post, and finding the door of his prison-house unfastened, owing to some unaccountable neglect, gravely walked out to take a more extended survey of matters and things on deck.

He seemed to find them much to his liking, and was taking a stroll to the lee side of the quarter-deck, looking as big as a newly-created millionaire, when Mr. Smeaton espied him. He was surprised to see the favorite bird strutting about at liberty, and alarmed lest he should be lost, immediately began to devise measures for his capture. He commanded every man to remain motionless, and not say a word, and slowly crept aft himself, at the same time making a sign to Peter Flam, the man at the helm, to come forward in the same stealthy manner, and be prepared to lay violent hands on the fugitive fowl when off his guard.

This mode of proceeding was shrewdly devised, and might, perhaps, have been carried into successful execution, had not another actor come forward, whose part was not in the programme, and who, to the inexpressible indignation of the second mate, exploded the whole of his plan just as it was being carried into effect.

Mark Rowland happened to be in the cabin at this time, and, of course, knew nothing of what was taking place on deck. He was called upon by Mr. Jarls, and directed to go up and ask Mr. Smeaton about the ship's course.and rate of sailing during the morning watch, which the second mate had neglected to record on the log-slate. Mark rushed up the companion-way in his usual lively and energetic manner, and turning short round to leeward, came almost in contact with the rooster just as Peter Flam had stretched out his hand to grab the foolish bird by the leg !

The result was an unfortunate one. The bird, frightened out of all propriety, uttered a sharp cry, half cackle and half crow, and spreading his wings, and giving a convulsive start, with a hop, step, and jump, rose from the deck, just cleared the quarter-rail, flew off fifteen or twenty yards from the ship, and alighted on the water, in which unenviable position, apparently ashamed and alarmed at the strange mistake he had made, he looked towards the ship as if beseeching to be taken on board again.

But the wrath of the second officer, when he saw the rooster take wing and fly overboard, was overpowering, and poor Mark was doomed to feel the brunt of his indignation. "You idle, good-for-nothing monkey," said he, "you have driven overboard a bird worth more than all your tribe. I never saw a cabin-boy yet that earned his salt. They always do ten times more mischief than they are worth ; and for two coppers, I would kick you overboard to follow the bird."

4

Mark was astonished, and greatly hurt, at receiving this unmerited broadside. He looked hard at the mate, then over the side of the ship upon the smooth water, and then at the rooster buoyantly resting on its surface. He was a good swimmer, having practised during the summer months in Rhadamanthus Pond, a dark sheet of water situated but a quarter of a mile from his mother's dwelling. It occurred to him that if he had, although unconsciously, been the cause of such a mighty piece of mischief as was represented by Mr. Smeaton, his proper course would be to recover the lost bird, and thus expiate the fault committed. And merely nodding to the officer, as much as to say, "I will make it all right, sir, directly," he jumped upon the taffrail, plunged head foremost into the water, and with lusty strokes began to swim away towards the bird.

Mr. Smeaton recovered his senses when he saw Mark mount the taffrail, and commanded him in a loud voice to step down. But it was too late. Mr. Jarls, hearing the various noises, betokening something serious, came rushing on deck, closely followed by the captain. Some of the sailors seeing Mark in the water, shouted, "A man overboard!" which roused all hands on deck in a hurry. Mr. Jarls ordered the helm to be put hard down, the tacks and bowlines to be let go, and the yards squared, to stop the ship's progress. The captain ordered the stern-boat to be cleared away and lowered, and greatly alarmed at Mark's foolhardiness, called aloud to him, "Come back, Mark, come back! Never mind the fowl! Come back, or you'll be drowned!"

Altogether there was a wonderful commotion suddenly conjured up on the decks of the Saladin.

Mark, who could not conceive of the possibility of danger in swimming in such smooth water, kept on his course to secure the fowl, now some fifteen or twenty fathoms from

the ship.   The stern-boat was lowered with all possible dispatch, and Mr. Jarls sprang into it, with a couple of sailors,
who seized the oars and began to pull towards the cabin-
boy, when all at once a large, dark-looking object shot out
from beneath the ship, rose nearly to the surface, and swam
swiftly away, following in the wake of Mark Rowland.

"A shark! a shark!" exclaimed the sailors, in a tone of
horror.

"God have mercy on the poor boy!" said Captain Somers; " but I fear 'tis all over with him.   Mr. Jarls," he continued, hailing the mate, " do you see the shark? Give way,
men, and save the poor fellow from the monster's jaws. Mr.
Jarls, seize the boat-hook, and fight him off."

. The mate had seen the shark, and the men were pulling
with all their strength; but the shark took the lead, paying
no attention to the boat, and Mr. Jarls, acting on the suggestion of Captain Somers, seized the boat-hook, a staff
some six or eight feet long, with a hook and a stout spike at
the end.   He now took his stand in the bow, and gave directions to the men how to pull.   Meanwhile Mark, utterly
unconscious of his danger, intent only on capturing the
fowl, had nearly reached the fugitive, and slackened his
efforts with a view to lay his hand gently upon him.   This
gave a fine opportunity for the shark, which had now ranged
alongside the cabin-boy, to seize upon his prey, — an opportunity which he did not neglect.   The ferocious animal
turned over on his side, that he might more conveniently
snap off one or both of the legs, which, in a very appetizing
manner, were dangling in the water.

But the boat came thundering on, with Mr. Jarls, a stout,
muscular man, in the bow, with a formidable weapon in his
hands.   Just as the shark had assumed a convenient attitude, and was about to take the first bite from the tempting
repast which chance had thrown in his way, the spike of the

boat-hook came down on the side of his devoted head, crashed through the bones, and doubtless penetrated the brain. The shark acknowledged the force of the blow by leaping nearly out of water, then swam off rapidly with the boat-hook sticking in his cranium, pursuing a very crooked course, and finally disappeared altogether in the depths below!

Mark was picked up and taken on board, and also the foolish fowl, which had been the cause of so much trouble, and which, by Captain Somers's orders, was handed over to the steward to furnish, the next day, a sea-pie for the cabin dinner. Mark was rebuked by the captain for his folly in jumping overboard at sea, under any circumstances, and admonished to stick by the ship in all weathers; and having been greatly startled when told of his narrow escape from the shark, he faithfully promised that he would never again expose himself to such a danger, unless to save the life of a fellow-creature.

That evening, in the dog-watch, the startling incidents of the day were fully discussed on the quarter-deck and on the forecastle. Captain Somers referred to the well-known case of the British man-of-war in Port Royal, Jamaica. This ship had occasion to lay at anchor in the harbor a long time, and the captain, finding his men frequently deserting by swimming ashore during the night, tolled the sharks around by feeding them occasionally with choice morsels of food. One of these sharks, of great size and ferocity, known as "Big Tom," was particularly vigilant as a guard, prowling around at all hours, within sight of the ship, and gobbling up sailor after sailor in their attempts to escape by swimming from the horrors of a British man-of-war. But unfortunately Big Tom could not be taught to distinguish between friend and foe, and he finally lost the confidence of the captain, who even persecuted him to death because the stupid

brute one evening gobbled up the captain's son, a young
"middy," who, being more than half drunk, fell overboard
while getting out of the boat alongside. And but little sympathy did the captain get from the crew for the loss of his
son.

"The narrow escape which Mark Rowland had to-day
from the jaws of a shark," said Mr. Jarls to Captain Somers, "reminds me of an incident of a similar character,
which I once witnessed in Manilla, when I was a sailor on
board the ship Vashti, belonging to Newburyport. One Sunday, while the ship was lying at anchor at Cavite, a portion
of the crew had liberty to go ashore, and, as is too often the
case, when they came on board in the afternoon, some of
them were greatly the worse for liquor, and of course partially bereft of reason, transformed for the time from rational
beings into brutes. Among these was an old salt, who went
by the name of Dan Colwell. He came on board in another
ship's boat, about four o'clock, crazy drunk, and stormed
about the deck, making great noise and confusion, until
compelled to go below by the officers.

"A few minutes after Dan Colwell went below, a large
shark made his appearance not far from the ship, slowly
moving about just beneath the surface of the water, with his
back fin and the upper part of his tail sticking out, as if
to warn all living creatures in that neighborhood to be on
their guard. His appearance, of course, caused no little
excitement. There was much running about the decks, loud
inquiries made for the shark-hook, harpoon, &c., and suggestions about getting ready a running bowline.

"Dan Colwell, who had been persuaded by his shipmates
to turn in, in order to sleep off the effect of his strong pota-
tions, no sooner heard the word 'shark,' than he rolled out
of his berth, and followed his shipmates on deck.

"'Where is the man-eating rascal?' cried Dan. 'Let

4*

me come at him. I am just in the trim to astonish him, —
to cut him up into minced meat, or slit him into strips for a
lobscouse!' So saying, he opened his large jack-knife,
which hung by a laniard around his neck, and, before his
shipmates could prevent him, or indeed guess what was his
intention, he threw himself over the gunwale into the water,
and struck out boldly towards the sea-monster, that was
plainly in sight, swimming away some twenty or thirty
yards off.

"The shark, hearing the splash in the water, turned
round, and after a sort of inquiring pause, began to swim
slowly towards the ship. He soon espied Dan, and quick-
ened his motions, probably with the expectation of making
a hearty meal of a tough old sailor.

"The crew, of course, were greatly alarmed at the danger which threatened their drunken shipmate, and clamorously insisted on his coming back to the ship. But Dan was
obstinate, and kept on his course, and before anything could
be done by those on board for his succor, the shark was
by his side, and fixed upon him his glittering eye, and seemed
in a very loving mood.

"The poor fellow's senses, which had been wandering,
suddenly resumed their usual functions. He became sober
as if by magic, and realized his danger to its full extent.
He knew that his own folly or madness had placed him in a
most perilous position. He turned and swam towards the
ship, exerting all the strength of which he was master. He
was closely followed by the shark, which animal, it is well
known, will seldom or never attack a man while vigorously
swimming or moving about in the water, as he has to turn
on his side before he can seize his prey, owing to the peculiar
construction of his jaws.

"Dan Colwell, in an agony of alarm, cried out right earnestly for help. 'Oh, Mr. Hardoc, save me from the shark! Help! help! help!'

"His screams and appeals for help were heard all over the harbor, but there was little chance for help at that particular time. The small boat was ashore with the captain, and the long boat was on the other side and without oars, which were quietly reposing on the deck of the ship, and help to be effective must be immediate. The chief mate, however, was a man of great presence of mind, and his resources in an emergency seemed inexhaustible. He called to the steward to hand him the musket from the cabin. This musket was one of a dozen clumsy-looking but formidable weapons, put on board for defence in case of an attack from pirates. It had been recently used by the captain in shooting gulls and other water fowl, on the passage, and was now standing in a corner of the cabin, loaded with a heavy charge of powder and swan shot.

"The musket was almost instantly passed into the hands of the mate, who, with wonderful dexterity, drew out the heavy iron ramrod, picked a ropeyarn from the deck and wound it around the end, and then thrust it into the barrel of the gun. He cocked the gun, and pointing it in the direction of Dan Colwell and his companion, held himself in readiness to act. All this passed in a much quicker period of time than it requires to relate it.

"In the mean while Dan was swimming back to the ship, his features distorted with terror, and still roaring for help, and the shark sticking to him closer than a brother. The second mate stood by with the harpoon, ready to make war upon the shark. One of the men had armed himself with the five-pronged grainse, and assumed a hostile attitude. Men also stood ready to lend a hand in the rescue of their shipmate, some in the main chain-wales, and some on deck, with ropes and poles, bowlines and buoys.

"Dan had nearly reached the side of the ship, and was about grasping a bowline which one of his shipmates had thrown to him to clap round his waist, when the shark, determined not to be cheated out of his prey, placed himself in a position to take the first mouthful of such a tempting morsel.

"And now all the ropes and bowlines and boats and shouts in the world would have little availed Dan Colwell, and he would have been food for a fish, perhaps for fishes, if Mr. Hardoc had not taken deliberate aim at the sea-monster, and pulled the trigger just as he was showing his glistening teeth. The noise of the gun, and the shot striking the water around the shark, must have astonished him greatly, but the iron ramrod, which passed right through his body, did more. The monster abandoned his prey, floundered about a few minutes, seeming bewildered, and then probably sank to the bottom, for we saw him no more.

"Dan Colwell was taken on board, more dead than alive. I never saw a man so terribly frightened in my life. He dropped on his knees as soon as he reached the deck, and devoutly thanked God for saving him from the jaws of the shark, and he took a solemn oath on the spot that he would never taste a drop of spirituous liquors again, and I have reason to believe that he kept his word."

CHAPTER IV.

WHILE the officers were busily engaged on the quarter-deck in discussing the subject of sea-monsters, a subject suggested by the events of the day, the men belonging to the watch, cosily seated on the spare spars under the lee of the long-boat, took up another subject of equal interest, which was also suggested by those occurrences. They spoke of the evil consequences of jumping overboard, and swimming away from the ship, even during a calm at sea, and related several cases where fatal results had ensued from thus indulging in a foolish whim or a frolicsome disposition.

"You are right, shipmates," said Sam Welkin, an old sailor, of a robust frame, with a grave countenance and quiet habits, who talked a great deal, talked well, too, but had hitherto been an attentive listener to the conversation. "A man should stick to his ship, whether it blows high or blows low; and when on the broad ocean, or thumping against a rock-bound shore in a gale of wind, should never abandon his ship for a moment and trust to his skill in swimming."

"But suppose he tumbles into the big pond by accident?" inquired Jack Manwell.

"He could not meet with worse luck!" said Sam Welkin, with a shudder. "But that will not be *his* fault, and he must do the best he can, with the chances terribly against his ever lounging on a ship's forecastle, or getting a glimpse

45

of an old landmark or light-house again. Did *you* ever fall overboard at sea, Jack?"

"Never, shipmate," replied Jack. "I never met with such bad luck. I was jerked off the foretop-sail yard one dark night, while reefing top-sails on board the brig Tarantula in the Bay of Biscay, bound to Bordeaux; and while one of my shipmates, poor fellow, who was on the lee yard-arm, was tossed into the water some dozen fathoms from the ship's side, and was never heard of afterwards, I was gently landed in the foretop, with only a sprained wrist and a bruised figure-head."

"When I was in the ship Dagon, bound to Greenock, and lying to under bare poles off the Isle of Sable," said a hard-looking old sailor, named Jason, "we shipped a sea which swept the deck, and washed overboard the second mate and the whole larboard watch, who all went to Davy's locker except myself, and I was saved only by being entangled in the fore-sheet, which nearly twisted off my starboard flipper before I got on board. And shipmates, it was sad to see them poor fellows in the ship's wake, broad off on the weather-quarter, before they went down, rising on the top of the waves, and stretching out their arms toward us, as if asking for aid which could not be given."

"Aye, such things are sad to witness," said Jack Manwell. "But I suppose they are all right. A man that goes to sea must expect to meet with squalls now and then. He can't expect to sail always in smooth water; otherwise, d'ye see, everybody would want to be a sailor, so we should be thankful for our lot such as it is, and not grumble at a hard chance."

Mark Rowland had crept in among the sailors, and was an eager listener to their conversation. He was much impressed by the remarks made by Sam Welkin, and the feeling manner in which they were delivered; and he interrupted the pause which followed Jack's philosophical reflections, by turning to Sam Welkin, and plumply asking the question, " Did *you* ever fall overboard at sea, Sam?"

" Once, and only once," replied the case-hardened old sailor; " but I did not take it so kindly as Jack Manwell is disposed to; and while I was in the water with no expectation of getting out, I am afraid I grumbled a little at my hard luck. And you may rely on my word, shipmates, that it is a fearful thing for a man to be floating on the ocean buoyed up by a plank, a spar, or a life-buoy, with no vessel in sight, and not one chance in a thousand that he will ever see a human face again, or grasp a shipmate by the hand. At such a time a man thinks fast, and in one hour lives half a century. He looks back upon his past life, and well for him if it is free from twists and crooks and kinks. His sufferings are terrible. I would not wish my worst enemy to be in his mess."

" How happened you to fall overboard, Sam?" inquired Mark Rowland. " I *do* wish you would tell us all about it?"

" Aye, give us the whole yarn, old fellow," said Jack Manwell; " we are all longing to have it twisted. What say ye, shipmates?"

A hearty response in the affirmative settled the question. Sam Welkin acceded to the wishes of his friends, and, in his loftiest style, — for he was something of a scholar, and could repeat half of " Falconer's Shipwreck " without looking into the book, and two thirds of Coleridge's " Ancient Mariner," — favored them with the following narrative, illustrative of the perilous incidents which chequer the life of a sailor.

" About eighteen years ago I shipped as a sailor on board the brig Silkworm, Captain Biffin, bound on a voyage from New York to Gibraltar and a market. We had been about a fortnight on the passage and were nearly half way across the Atlantic, when one evening, just after dark, a black cloud suddenly appeared on the weather-quarter, and came rapidly towards us. The captain, who was on deck, ordered the light sails to be taken in, and the flying-jib having been hauled down, I passed out over the bowsprit to furl it. I reached the flying jib-boom, and had just gathered in the sail in readiness to pass the gasket, when the squall struck the brig. It came with a sudden gust; the sail, light as it was, flapped heavily, caught me around the head, and twisted me over the boom, so that before I could clutch the jib-stay, guy, or any other rope, I fell from the jib-boom into the water.

"The ship, dashing onward, passed directly over me, but I came to the surface when I got in the wake, and puffed and blowed like a porpoise to recover my breath. I could swim like a seal, and did not at first realize the danger of my position. I looked around for the ship, and cloudy as it was, could see her distinctly, and also hear the shouts on board, 'A man overboard! Welkin has fallen from the jib-boom!' was repeated fore and aft.

"Captain Biffin was a kind-hearted man. He was all alive on this occasion. He instantly gave orders in a loud and decided tone. 'Hard down the helm! hard down! Clear away the stern-boat! Be handy, men, and save the poor fellow's life! Throw over the booby-hatch! Throw over a hen-coop! Square away the main-yard.'

"Now, mounting the taffrail, the captain called out in a clear and encouraging voice, and every syllable he uttered I heard with the utmost distinctness, for at such a time, shipmates, a man's senses are all wide awake: 'Keep up your spirits, Sam! Don't be discouraged! The boat will be alongside of you in no time!'"

"The booby-hatch and a hen-coop were tossed overboard the moment the alarm was given, and while I was but a short distance astern of the ship. I attempted to get hold of one of them, knowing that my only chance was, not in trying to swim towards the brig, but in reserving my strength to keep my head above water until the boat could be lowered and manned and sent to my relief. After swimming about for a few minutes I got hold of the booby-hatch, to which I clung as closely as a sucker-fish will cling to the back of a shark.

" The brig going through the water seven or eight knots when the squall struck her, was at least a quarter of a mile off before her way could be stopped and the boat lowered; and even when the brig was rounded to, she continued to drift to leeward faster than a man could swim in smooth water. Clinging to the booby-hatch, which, as you know, shipmates, is something like an open box, six or eight feet square and a couple of feet deep, and made of light pine plank, I could keep my head out of the water most of the time without any great effort, and thus had opportunity and leisure to work a traverse in my own mind, and find out how the chances stood.

" It was now nearly dark, and I knew I could not be seen from the ship, if indeed I had been seen at all, after having fallen overboard; and at that moment I earnestly prayed to God that the boat might be pulled towards the spot where I was floating on the water. I shuddered when I thought that, in the darkness, the boat's crew might not know in what direction to steer, and after looking around a while, and not finding me, might suppose I was drowned, and go back to the ship, leaving me to my fate.

" I saw the boat put off from the ship. I saw the dark object as it approached. My heart fluttered with hope, but soon sunk within me as the men ceased rowing, while the boat was still at a distance. I could hear the shouts of the men calling out my name, as they rose faintly above the murmur of the waves around me. I tried to answer the

5

glad sounds, and attract attention by shouts louder than their own, but my voice was weak and hoarse, either through exhaustion by swimming or by swallowing a double allowance of salt water, and I soon became aware, to my great dismay, that in spite of my utmost exertions I could not make myself heard by the men in the boat.

"The boat came no nearer, but went off on another course, and then came back towards me, the men continuing at intervals to call out my name, and then they pulled round and round, and backwards and forwards, several times. It was a moment of maddening suspense. I exerted, but in vain, all my powers of voice and limb to telegraph to my shipmates that I was still alive, and alive like to be, within hail, and almost within their reach, and by a slight effort on their part could be picked up and carried on board the brig. But although they often appeared to listen, they could not hear my voice, which the more I tried to raise it — as if hailing the deck from the maintop-mast cross-trees in a pampero — the more I felt it sounded faint, hoarse, and asthmatic, as if a grape-shot was lodged in my throat.

"I will do Mr. Caswell, the second mate, and my shipmates who were with him in the boat, the justice to say that they exerted themselves manfully, and did all that could have been expected from sailors of the true blue stamp, to find my course and bearings on that memorable evening, but they could not do it."

"Could not do it?" exclaimed Mark Rowland, in a tone of wonder. "Did not the boat's crew find you before you were entirely exhausted, and take you on board?"

"No," replied Sam, resuming his narrative, "a light was now displayed from the ship, and a musket was fired as a signal for the boat to return; and lads, you may imagine the horror which froze my blood, when the conviction was forced upon me that the boat had abandoned the search and was returning to the ship. With straining eyeballs I still gazed in the direction of the vessel on whose decks I lately trod, and threw my hands towards her in agony, madly entreating, in hoarse whispers, for that help which I knew now I should not receive. Through the shadows of night I could see the dark mass in the distance gradually growing more and more indistinct, until it was entirely lost to my view.

"And now I was in the midst of the wide ocean, floating on the waves, alone! A dreadful solitude, with certain death staring me in the face. My brain seemed to whirl round, my head was giddy, and I was sick at heart, when I realized my condition. After a time I recovered my reason to a certain extent, and actually began to speculate on my fate! I tried to calculate how long I should hold out, hanging on to that float in the water; whether the wind would rise, and the waves angrily dash over me and soon end my sufferings, or whether, overcome by fatigue and sleep, I should release my grip, and sink quietly beneath the waves. Perhaps it would be my lot to die a slow death by starvation.

"While indulging in these speculations I felt a strange curiosity and earnest desire to know what would become of me, — not merely the manner of my death, but my destination after death. Should I be punished dreadfully and eternally for the many sins I had committed on earth, or would the Lord, in his infinite mercy, taking into view the few chances I had of improving my mind and morals, and the many temptations that had beset me on every side, forgive my sins and take me to his bosom? At that hour, shipmates, which I considered my dying hour, I heartily repented of all my sins.

"Then again a gleam of hope would flit across my mind. My situation was not so bad but that it might have been worse. I had something to cling to, which, should the weather continue moderate, would aid me to float a long time on the water, and my heart throbbed with pleasure, when the idea flashed across my mind that if I could hold on until the next morning, it was possible some vessel might cross that spot and extend a helping hand.

"But when I reflected that but few vessels took that track across the ocean, and that even if one passed within a quarter of a mile, the chances were a thousand to one against my being seen, my float being even with the water, and no signal being displayed. I again abandoned all hope, and could hardly help regretting that my life was prolonged. I felt a strong impulse, which I could hardly resist, to quit my booby-hatch, and put an end to this terrible state of suspense and uncertainty.

"Then fortitude would come to my aid, and I resolved, desperate as my condition was, to struggle for life as long as I could move a muscle, and stave off to the most distant period possible the hour of death. For oh, shipmates, life is sweet. Though sometimes we meet with rough weather, head winds, squalls, typhoons, and hurricanes on the voyage, we more frequently meet with prosperous breezes and un-ruffled seas. There are joys and comforts as well as troubles in this world, and as to the future — who knows what will be its character? Not a poor ignorant sailor like myself!

"And then I thought of my home, of my childhood, when I rambled through the woods and pastures, happy in the present and looking forward to joy in the future. I thought of my parents, of my kind and loving mother, my brothers and sisters, none of whom I had seen for years, but who never seemed so near and dear as at that moment when I was about to land on the dark shores of another world.

"But it is impossible to tell all which passed through my mind on that terrible night — a night so long that I feared it would never end. My nerves were sadly out of tune, my heart beat violently, and my brain throbbed with excitement. If I should live for ages, I shall never forget it. How rapidly I thought! How clear and distinct were my recollections! My whole life with its many incidents, and every person with whom I had ever associated, or in whose welfare I had felt any interest, passed in review before me!

" Hours passed away. The wind continued light, and the sea comparatively smooth. The stars shone with unusual brilliancy. The waves no longer broke over me as if impatient to engulf me; and as I partly rested my body on the buoyant hatchway, which rose and fell with the ocean swell, and upon the sides of which I retained a firm grasp with my fingers, I actually fell into a doze, and, unlikely as it may seem, was for a while unconscious of the horrors of my situation.

When I awoke the streaks of early dawn were visible in the east, and I eagerly watched the approach of day to cast an eye around the horizon. Having been so wonderfully preserved for many hours, I was led to indulge a faint, but hardly acknowledged hope that I should be rescued from the waves by some passing vessel.

" As daylight advanced, I could see to a considerable distance in every direction. No object met my view but the sky above and the dark waters around and beneath me. The last spark of hope was extinguished, and I made up my mind to meet my fate like a man.

" But just as the sun rose above the horizon, an object in the west caught my eye, which reflected the rays of the sun, and shone like a white speck afar off. I at once knew it was a ship, and my heart swelled again with expectation and hope. I kept my eyes steadily fixed on that object, anxious to know the course it was steering, and by its rapidly increasing size, I soon knew it was approaching!

5*

" My eyes were riveted on that vessel. It was not long
before I could count her sails, and see between her masts.
The ship was on a wind steering to the north-east, and if she
kept on that course would pass me at least a couple of miles
to the northward. I watched her course with intense interest. Every manœuvre, every change, every motion, was
closely noted, and I fervently prayed that some circumstance
might occur to bring her within hail. An hour passed, and
she kept on in the same direction. My hopes again vanished. But suddenly the wind hauled to the northward and
headed the ship off a couple of points, and to my great joy
she was put about on the other tack, and headed almost
directly towards me !

"As the ship approached, the wind became unsteady.
Sometimes I was on her weather-bow, sometimes on her lee-
bow, and sometimes directly ahead. No one can imagine
the agony of my suspense as I watched that vessel. As she
drew near, and steering almost a straight course for my
booby-hatch, a flaw of wind struck her and headed her off a
couple of points, enough to carry her in a few minutes past
me, and beyond the reach of my voice. Knowing this was
my only chance, that ' now or never' was the word, I left
the kind float which had so long borne me above the waves,
and struck off in a course which would carry me ahead of
the ship. Fortunately for me the wind was now light, and
the ship was no clipper, and I soon reached my station
directly in her hawse, which I felt would enable me to speak
her, if she kept on her course.

" By this time I had recovered the full tone of my voice,
and as soon as I thought I could be heard by the men on her
decks, I began to hail, ' Ship ahoy ! ship ahoy ! throw me
a rope !'

" I hailed several times, and was nearly alongside to leeward before I could make them understand that a poor lost

sailor was in the sea, and bellowing for help. I was disgusted with their stupidity. At length the man at the helm
heard me, and after looking around for a few seconds, he
said in a sleepy tone, 'Captain Dace, Captain Dace, I—I
—believe, somebody, or—something—is hailing the ship
there to leeward!'

"The captain, mate, and all hands rushed to the side of
the ship at this startling announcement, so lazily given, and
were greatly astonished and frightened at seeing my ugly-
looking figure-head sticking up out of the water, and hearing
me, in passable English, call out to them not to stand there
idly staring at a sailor adrift, but to bear a hand and send a
boat, for I had had swimming enough to last me my lifetime, and wanted to be taken on board!

"This brought them to their senses, and it no sooner
flashed upon their minds that I was no marine monster, but
a poor fellow-creature in distress, than the captain, in his
excitement, took off his hat, waved it around his head, and
threw it overboard, at the same time giving orders to 'square
the main-yard!' The men gave three cheers, the most welcome sounds I ever heard in my life, and sprung to their
work. The ship's way was stopped, the quarter-boat was
lowered, and in less than five minutes I was on board the
ship Coquille, Captain Richard Dace, bound from Providence
to Gibraltar and a market.

"And shipmates, I was treated in the kindest manner on
board this ship, supplied with clothes, and made comfortable
in every way. But the Coquille being a dull sailer, we were
a long time in reaching Gibraltar, and on the afternoon on
which we entered the bay we espied a brig coming out of
the harbor and steering for the Mediterranean. This brig
was the Silkworm, the same old craft from whose flying jib-
boom I tumbled into the sea some five weeks before. I
recognized her at once, and told Captain Dace, who hoisted

a signal, ran down towards her, and hailing her, asked the captain to heave to for a few minutes, as he wanted to send a boat on board.

"Captain Biffin complied with the request, wondering what the stranger wanted. The boat was manned. I shook hands with Captain Dace, his officers, and the whole ship's company, and wished them endless prosperity, for if I had been a brother they could not have treated me more kindly. I took my seat in the stern of the boat, and in a few minutes was alongside the brig. I bade my kind friends in the boat good-by, stepped into the main-chainwales, and sprang lightly over the gunwale to the main-deck and into the midst of the group of officers and men who were gathered there, curious to know what was the trouble. I stared Captain Biffin full in the face, took off my hat, and, scratching my head, said, in the most respectful manner, " I have come aboard, sir, at last ! '

" I never saw a man so astonished as Captain Biffin was when he caught my eye as I was coming over the gunwale. He turned as pale as an iceberg, and stepped back a pace or two, as if he had seen a ghost. But when I took off my hat and he heard my voice, he exclaimed, ' It *is* Sam Welkin, as sure as there's snakes in Virginny. Boys,' he continued, turned to the wondering crew, ' here's your old shipmate, Sam Welkin, come aboard again safe and sound. He has managed by some means to get to windward of Davy Jones, after all ! '

" The men gave three rousing hurrahs, which fairly shook the old brig, and one after another grasped my hand as if determined to twist my arm off. The captain now gave the order to ' fill away the maintop-sail,' in which work, notwithstanding my exposure and fatigue and weakness, after having been soaked so long in salt water, I willingly lent a hand, and in half an hour, having rounded 'the Rock,' we were sailing merrily up the Mediterranean!"

So ended the yarn which Sam Welkin reeled off to his admiring shipmates. But all good-natured comments or sharp criticisms, which might have been expected from his auditors, were prevented; for he had hardly got through when the man at the helm called out "Eight bells!", and the officer of the deck gave the glad order, " Call the watch!"

CHAPTER V.

As the Saladin reached the tropical latitudes, and was quietly urged onwards by the light trade-winds, Mark Rowland was astonished at the vast numbers of flying-fish which frequented that part of the ocean. They reminded him of the story he had heard of a boy who, having returned from a voyage to the West Indies, was amusing his grandmother with false or exaggerated accounts of wonders he had seen. But when he began to tell about flying-fish, the good old lady cut short his stories at once by saying, " That's enough, Tom. Your talk about rivers of rum and mountains of sugar I believed, because such things are possible ; but as for flying-fish, I don't believe a syllable about them ! "

Sometimes these fish, with wings which they never flap, would rise several feet out of the water in flocks of fifty or a hundred, and after skimming along over the waves a distance of fifteen or twenty fathoms, drop into their native element, and were seen no more. And often in the night, when there was a breeze, a flock of flying-fish on the wing, not aware that there was a large, unwieldly monster in the shape of a ship in their immediate neighborhood, would strike against the weather-side of the Saladin, and perhaps a half dozen, and sometimes a dozen, of these curious and interesting inhabitants of the deep would be wafted over the gunwale, and fall on the deck, furnishing a breakfast next morning for the inmates of the cabin, for which an epicure would pawn his most costly jewel.

Where there are many flying-fish dolphins are also often met with, and the winged fishes constitute an important article of food for the larger inhabitants of the deep. Mark Rowland was deeply interested in watching the motions and habits of these animals, the pursuer and the pursued, the ruthless destroyer and his victim. His sympathies, being always warmly enlisted in behalf of the persecuted flying-fish, he would sometimes go out on the bowsprit, and seating himself in the forestay-sail netting, keep his eye on the dolphin, while the scaly tyrant was prowling around in search of his prey.

This beautiful but ferocious fish would gently and quietly draw near the bows of the ship, but generally keeping far enough off to be out of danger from the grainse or any other offensive weapon, then apparently motionless, without moving a fin, he would swim along, keeping exactly in the same relative position, all the time looking ahead, intent on mischief. All at once he would dart forward swifter than any race-horse starting from his post; and at the same moment a flock of flying-fish, terrified and fearing for their lives, would rise and shoot along over the surface of the water with great velocity, until their strength was exhausted. But when these persecuted creatures dropped into the water their mortal enemy, who had kept pace with them in their flight, was there, directly beneath them, ready and eager to snap them up, one after another, until his appetite was satisfied. Indeed, seldom is a dolphin taken in those latitudes without finding within him several flying-fish which were just entombed. These are carefully preserved in pickle, to be used for bait, and in their turn become the means of destroying the enemies of their race!

One afternoon Mark Rowland went aloft, as he was apt to do, to take a look round the horizon and across the water, to learn what was going on in old Neptune's dominions. Not a vessel or a wreck was in sight, nor did he see any unfortunate sailor clinging to a booby-hatch. But on looking on the water nearer the ship, he saw two dolphins of large size, a few fathoms from the ship on the lee-bow, swimming along very lovingly together.

"Hallo!" quoth Mark to himself. "A pair of dolphins! Husband and wife, perhaps. Who knows? I wonder if fishes have kind feelings towards each other, and cultivate tender affections!"

He hurried down on deck, resolved to try his hand and his luck in capturing one or both of these unsuspecting strangers.

A fishing-line which had been unsuccessfully used the day before was lying coiled up on the deck, with a stout hook, and a flying-fish for bait attached. He said not a word to indicate that large fish were around, but kept his own counsel, with a view to have all the sport to himself. He seized upon the fishing-line, and before a man could say, "avast, there!" was at the jib-boom end, lowering his line into the water, and bobbing it up and down, his face glowing with excitement, and his eye sparkling with the pleasurable hope of luring one of those noble fish to dart at the hook, and finish his destructive career.

Nor was Mark mistaken in his calculation. The dolphins, evidently, unfamiliar with the various devices resorted to by man for their destruction, and seeing nothing particularly alarming in the appearance of the ship, a huge wooden monster, moving along steadily through the water, boldly made a rush at the hook the moment they saw it from a distance. One of them, the largest and probably the male, being a little in advance, seized it with avidity, and the next moment experienced a new and unpleasant sensation, the hook being strongly fastened in his lower jaw. He made frantic efforts to break loose from the cord, which, like a bond of fate, connected him with the cabin-boy on the bowsprit. He pulled and tugged, exerting all his strength he jerked and floundered, and leaped out of the water; but all would not do. He was firmly hooked, and struggled against his fate in vain.

Mark rejoiced in his success, and essayed to haul up his huge captive, take him in on deck and exhibit him to his shipmates as a proof of his adroitness and skill. But the dolphin, weighing nearly a hundred pounds, was too large for him to handle, and he was reluctantly compelled to call for help. He created quite a sensation by crying out, "Hallo, there on deck! I have hooked a dolphin! a big fellow! and cannot haul him up. Bring out the grainse, and be quick about it, or we shall lose him."

Mr. Jarls, hearing the outcry, went forward, and comprehended the case at once. He armed himself with the grainse, a death-dealing instrument, with five barbed prongs, and passed out on the bowsprit to the relief of Mark Rowland.

In the mean time Mark was witness to a scene which settled in his own mind the question with regard to the affections and kind feelings of those bloodless and heartless animals, supposed by many to be the very essence of stupidity and selfishness, known as fishes.

The companion of the dolphin which was hooked, undoubtedly a female, as soon as she became aware of the real state of the case, and was convinced that her companion had got himself into trouble, and that his liberty and life were in imminent danger, made the strongest possible manifestations of grief and alarm. Regardless of danger to herself, she swam quickly around and around the captive,

6

as if to ascertain the precise nature of his trouble, while he was struggling hard to break the line. Then she would swim off to a distance of several .fathoms, and return with wonderful velocity, throwing herself against the line, as if in the hope that what one could not accomplish might be effected by their united efforts. Then she would snap at the line with her teeth, but without doing it much injury, and in various ways exhibited her affection for her companion, pity for his sufferings, and indignation against his tormenters.

But this scene, which was watched by Mark with intense interest, was soon brought to a close by the promptness of Mr. Jarls. Having no faith in the sentimentality of fishes, he smiled grimly when Mark, in the simplicity of his heart, begged him to " spare them both, they were so fond of each other ! " He poised the fatal weapon, and selecting not the one already hooked, but his restless companion, planted the prongs of the grainse deeply in her back. The fish was soon transferred to the deck, and as soon as the grainse was disengaged from the quivering muscles, it was handed back, when he hurled it with the same success at the larger fish, which was still struggling convulsively to regain his freedom.

Mark's heart was sensibly touched by the scene he had witnessed. He pitied the unfortunate dolphins, and almost regretted that he had been instrumental in their capture. But when he recalled to mind their well-known voracity and their unsparing cruelty towards the flying-fish, which fish again feasted on fishes and aquatic animals, smaller than themselves, he became reconciled to the result, and partook with a good appetite of the " chowder for all hands," of which the dolphins formed the chief ingredient.

Mark had frequent opportunities afterwards to witness the wonderful peculiarities and sagacity of fishes, especially in

the amicable relations which ever exist between the pilot-
fish and the shark, — so unlike each other in size, habits,
and appearance. This strange tie of friendship between the
ravenous monster and the beautiful mottled little fish is not
a mere fable, as many believe, but a reality, and is described
more fully in the author's work, entitled "Jack in the Forecastle."

Sailors, as a general thing, are honest men. Although
not backward sometimes in relating improbable incidents,
and giving them the guise of truth, they hold a *liar* in abhor-
rence, and despise a *thief*. Indeed, it is seldom that a thief
is found on a ship's forecastle, and when found, the life he
leads is not a pleasant one.

On board the Saladin was a man named Peter, or Pedro,
who was no favorite with the officers or the rest of the crew.
He was a foreigner, of a dark, sallow complexion, and believed to be a Portuguese. He was ignorant and supersti-
tious, with principles and morals at low-water mark. He
was not much of a sailor, although he shipped for full
wages; and being constitutionally lazy, would shirk labor
whenever an opportunity offered. But being in Mr. Jarl's
watch, that vigilant officer, who was a great stickler for justice in the abstract, managed to screw out of Peter a much
greater amount of work, and that of no very desirable character, than the worthless fellow would willingly have performed.

One forenoon, while Jack Manwell was at the helm, and
Mr. Jarls was walking the quarter-deck, Jack, with a very
sober countenance, told the mate that, when he left Boston,
he had, in a secret drawer in his chest, twenty-five Spanish
dollars, a part of the wages received for his last voyage,
with which he meant to buy in Calcutta some kickshaws or
things, strange or beautiful, as presents to his friends in
Marblehead. "They were there, safe and sound, when I

overhauled my chest last Sunday," said Jack, with a sigh, "but now they are gone."

"Ah ha!" said the mate. "A thief on board! This is a serious matter. We must catch the rascal, and expose him. Do you suspect any one, Jack?"

"I don't believe there's a man on board would do such a dirty trick, unless it be that lazy, piratical-looking chap, with the snakish eyes,—that Peter."

"And what makes you suspect Peter, Jack?" said Mr. Jarls, with a sort of half-laugh.

"I have no proof, whatever," said Jack; "but he has had chances enough to do it if he wanted to. Besides, I know he's a liar, and a man who will lie will always steal."

"Admirable logic!" exclaimed the mate; "worthy of Harry Stotle himself. Say no more; keep quiet. If that scamp of a Peter has stolen it, we'll get it again, never fear."

Mr. Jarls, after a short consultation with Captain Somers, went forward, and summoning the sailors around him, said, "My men, Jack Manwell has had twenty-five dollars stolen from his chest within a few days. Now it is important to find out who is the thief, as well as to recover the money. No innocent man, of course, will object to having his chest searched at once. So I wish you all to hand me the keys, and the sooner this matter is settled, the better."

Every man whose chest was locked produced the key at once. Peter's was not locked. "He was not afraid," he said, "to trust to the honesty of his shipmates."

"That's more than your shipmates can say of you," said the mate.

Peter scowled, and looked marline-spikes.

Mr. Jarls searched every chest, and examined every berth, but no money could be found.

"Now," said he, "I'll go another way to work, — a way that I never knew fail. Come aft, all of you!"

The men followed the first officer aft to the capstan, which he made them surround. He then told every man to place the forefinger of his right hand on the edge of the capstan, which was done without hesitation, Peter alone showing symptoms of agitation, and looking as if he wished he was anywhere else.

"Now," said Mr. Jarls, in a tone befitting the serious occasion, "I will raise this hammer aloft, and say, ' *mene, mene, tekel, upharsin,*' and then bring it down with all my force upon the capstan, and it will be sure to fall upon the finger of the thief who stole the money, and smash it to atoms. So look out, men!" added he, raising the hammer; " *mene, mene* —— "

"Avast, there, Mr. Jarls!" screamed the terrified Peter, snatching his finger from the capstan. "I will confess all without having my finger smashed. The devil tempted me, and I stole the money."

"You did, did you?" exclaimed the mate, seizing him by the throat. "I thought so, you outlandish scoundrel. What did you do with the money? Bring it here, and lay it on the capstan, or overboard you go, in strict accordance with the laws of Neptune."

The miserable being, convicted on his own confession of a felonious crime, trembled like an aspen leaf; and as soon as Mr. Jarls released him from his grasp, Peter stripped himself of his outer garments, and after fumbling about his loins, produced a canvas belt which, on being ripped open, was found to contain twenty-five dollars, and several other small articles of value, which had mysteriously disappeared from the chests in the forecastle.

The inquisition was at an end. The thief had been found, and the money recovered. The men went forward in a body,

6*

Peter hanging behind, looking exceedingly anxious; for he saw the indignant glances of his shipmates, and was by no means sure that he should entirely escape the painful punishment which he knew he deserved.

And Peter had reason for his doubts, for no sooner had the men reached the forecastle than Sam Welkin said, " What shall we do with this fellow, this thief? It will never do to let him off so ! "

" By no means," said Nicholas Haxon. " If I had my' way, I would keel-haul him. It would be a good lesson. He would never steal afterwards."

" I believe you," said Ned Thrumbo. " But keel-hauling is a barbarous punishment. It would be better to give him a sea-toss at once. But there is a way by which we can show him and each other the detestation in which we hold the pitiful, sneaking, unsailor-like crime which he has been guilty of, *We must cobb him !* "

" That's it ! " shouted the men, in chorus. " Ned, you speak like an inspired grumpus or a second Jonah. We will cobb him."

And in spite of Peter's cries and entreaties he was seized forthwith, and tied firmly to the windlass-bitts, and compelled to undergo a species of corporal punishment which is exceedingly painful while being administered, but which leaves no disfiguring marks, and inflicts no permanent injury. In laying on the blows with the broad side of a heavy hand-saw, every man and the cook, also, participated in turn, so that, in case of a legal prosecution, no one could testify to facts without criminating himself. The poor wretch howled and screamed and writhed in agony. But this had no effect in softening the hearts of his indignant shipmates. He called for aid upon the captain and officers, but they wisely left the deck when they saw preparations for a righteous punishment going on, and, in the cabin, turning a deaf ear to his cries, let the men uninterruptedly go through with their good work.

As the ship Saladin drew towards the equinoctial line, light winds and calms prevailed. A long passage was threatened; and Captain Somers was anxious lest his fresh water should not hold out, as the men, in that extremely hot climate, not being put on allowance, drank an incredible quantity of water, and unless the casks could be filled by rains from the clouds, or some means devised to check the indulgence of the thirsty propensities of the crew, it would ere long be necessary to put them on very short allowance. In this emergency an expedient was adopted, which was attended with good results.

A can which held a large half pint, was placed in the fore-top-mast cross-trees, and when a man wanted to drink he was obliged to climb aloft, take possession of the tumbler, come down on deck, fill it to the brim once, if he chose, drink it off, and then carry the can back to the lofty height from which it was taken. Mr. Jarls, who was quite a mathematician, after taking great pains in the calculation, declared that the men when obliged to take so much trouble to get water, did not drink more than two fifths as much as they did when the water-cask was at hand, and they were allowed to drink out of a quart pot!

But it was not long necessary to continue this expedient, for one day in the latitude of about three degrees north, after a dead calm for eight and forty hours, heavy clouds were seen rising from every part of the horizon. Soon were seen the flashes of the forked lightning, while the mutterings of the distant thunder were heard. The dark clouds rapidly gathered in the zenith and seemed to pour out cataracts of fire, while the stunning claps of thunder, peal after peal, sounded in the ears of the crew of the Saladin, like the awful artillery of heaven!

And now the rain began to come down, not in large heavy drops, but in sheets. It was a continuous stream instead of a shower; or if a shower, such an one as was never experienced excepting in the neighborhood of the equator. All hands were called to "fill up the water-casks." The scuppers were stopped with swabs, and the rain-water was soon knee-deep on deck. Pails, pans, pots, and noggins, all were put in requisition. The empty casks were soon filled, and every vessel that would hold water also. Before the shower was over, and it did not last an hour, the Saladin was far better supplied with fresh water than when she left the wharf in Boston; and greatly to the gratification of the sailors the half-pint can was taken down from the cross-trees.

CHAPTER VI

AN UNTIMELY NAP.

THE ship Saladin, having been detained unusually long in these low latitudes by calms, was forced a considerable way out of her proper course by the strong current that continually sets to the westward in that part of the Atlantic which embraces a few degrees on each side of the equator, and gives the original impulse to that remarkable current, which pouring out of the Gulf of Mexico, and sweeping along the coast of the United States, is known as the Gulf Stream. Captain Somers was not aware of the strength of the current, for he had no chronometer, and had neglected to ascertain his longitude by lunar observations, and on the second morning after the inundating thunder-shower, which came so opportunely, soon after the sun rose above the horizon, he was greatly astonished to hear the cry of "Land ho!" from the mast-head.

This land proved to be the little island of Ponedo, or St. Paul, a barren, and of course uninhabited rock, rising to the height of one hundred or one hundred and fifty feet out of the sea, and situated about a degree north of the equator at a long distance from other land, being nearly midway between the continents of Africa and America.

The ship gradually drew towards the island, and the sea being smooth, the weather pleasant, and the light wind having died away, Captain Somers was induced to send Mr.

Smeaton, the second mate, ashore in the ship's yawl, with a boat's crew, and a good supply of fishing-tackle, to procure a stock of fresh fish and bird's eggs, as well as to explore the island. Mark Rowland earnestly begged permission to go in the boat, and the captain consented to his wish.

The boat shoved off, and in a short time reached the shore, which was hardly a mile off, in a south-western direction. Mr. Smeaton found little difficulty in landing from a small nook or cove in the western side of the island. And fine amusement the sailors had in clambering over the cliffs, picking up the eggs of sea-birds, frightening the birds themselves by their boisterous greeting, and taking shell-fish of various kinds from the rocks at the edge of the water.

Vegetation was scarce on the island, for there was little or no soil. A few scraggy bushes, and tufts of coarse grass grew in some of the cavities in the rocks; but the air was alive with birds, the only inhabitants, which screamed and scolded vociferously at being thus rudely disturbed, insulted, and robbed; and fish of different sizes and variegated colors, abounded in the waters which broke on its rugged shores, and kindly allowed themselves to be caught by the sailors, who stood on the rocks which hung over the water, and cast in their lines, to which were appended cod-hooks baited with tempting pieces of pork.

The calm continued, and there seemed no prospect of a breeze. The surface of the ocean looked like a gigantic mirror. Of course Mr. Smeaton saw no necessity for being in a hurry to terminate the exploration and return to the ship. He and the sailors enjoyed themselves for an hour and a half, not aware of the lapse of time. They had a regular frolic, — sung, danced, and shouted, and procured and placed in the boat a generous supply of fish and eggs of the sea-fowl, to say nothing of crabs, crawfish as big as lobsters, and periwinkles without number.

The sailors, having such a glorious time, were desirous to make the most of it, and all with the exception of Mark Rowland slowly and reluctantly assembled near the boat after Mr. Smeaton had more than once reminded them that it was time to go on board; and then their attention was attracted to the manœuvres of a large shark which had closely approached the rocks, aware that something was going on that might redound to his advantage. Perhaps he dreamed of making a dinner off the leg of a sailor.

While they still lingered on the rocks, they were suddenly awakened to a sense of their duty, by the sound of a gun; and Mr. Smeaton, on mounting the summit of a rock, whence he could obtain a survey of the ocean, saw the Saladin with her ensign flying, as a signal for the boat's crew to hasten on board. The reason for this signal was also seen, for in the east a dark squall was rapidly rising, and the flashes of lightning were already visible, followed ·by low mutterings of distant thunder.

Mr. Smeaton was greatly alarmed, for he well knew how suddenly the squalls make their appearance in these latitudes, and how fiercely they sometimes blow, although the tempest is usually short-lived. He upbraided himself for not keeping a more vigilant lookout, and ordered the men into the boat immediately. His orders were promptly obeyed, for the sailors had heard the signal-gun, and were anxious only to return to the ship. They scrambled into the boat in a hurry, seized the oars, shoved off, and were leaving the island, when Mr. Smeaton, to his great consternation, ascertained that the cabin-boy, Mark Rowland, was not among them. He had been entirely forgotten in the bustle of departure. Where was he?

The men were ordered to "back water, forthwith." Mr. Smeaton landed again, and with three of the sailors proceeded in search of the missing cabin-boy. They shouted his name repeatedly, but the shrill screams of the sea-gulls, were their only answer. They clambered over the craggy rocks, traversed the island, and examined the cavities and chasms, but no trace of Mark Rowland could be found. He had strangely disappeared, how, they knew not, but finally came to the melancholy conclusion that while venturing along the verge of same overhanging cliff, he had fallen down the precipice into the deep waters at its base, and was drowned.

While Mr. Smeaton and the boat's crew were speculating upon the mysterious fate of their young companion, but without relinquishing their search among the rocks, another gun from the ship attracted their attention, and reminded them of other duties. They all felt that, notwithstanding their reluctance to quit the island until every nook and cranny had been thoroughly searched, hopeless as such a task appeared to be, they must not tarry longer, but hasten on board the ship, as the squall was coming up with giant strides, and presenting a threatening aspect. They knew that if they lost time, and neglected to ply their oars lustily to get on board before the tempest struck the ship, the chances were decidedly against their ever treading the decks of the Saladin. They therefore reluctantly abandoned the poor cabin-boy to his fate, and making strenuous efforts, succeeded in getting alongside just before the squall, bearing with it sheets of rain and mist and furious gusts of wind, struck the ship with a mighty force, throwing her over nearly on her beam-ends.

There was no time for asking questions or relating occurrences. Every man was obliged to take hold and work with a will, and for a time the fate of Mark Rowland remained untold. Before the boat could be hoisted to the quarter-davits, the storm was upon them in all its fury. The wind blew a hurricane for a time, threatening to tear the canvas from the bolt-ropes. The rain fell in torrents, and it was found necessary to keep the ship off the wind, and let her scud before the tempest.

Long before the sun had sunk beneath the horizon the gale had spent its fury, the dark clouds had dispersed, and the Saladin was running merrily along to the southward, under the influence of a fine breeze from the eastward, at the rate of seven or eight knots. Yet one of that ship's company, who in the morning was with them, joyous and happy, was missing. Mark Rowland, the cabin-boy, whose courage, energy, and amiable disposition had made him beloved by every inmate of the cabin or forecastle, was no longer on board, and the little islet of Ponedo was no longer visible in the horizon.

When the misfortune which had happened to Mark was made known by Mr. Smeaton, a gloom was spread over the whole ship's company. From the circumstances as detailed it was clear, beyond the shadow of a doubt, that Mark was no longer in the land of the living. His fate was deeply regretted by Captain Somers, as the interesting cabin-boy was commended to his particular care by Mr. Fortesque, the owner of the ship. The captain severely rebuked Mr. Smeaton for lingering so long on the island, and neglecting to look closely after the men under his charge. He deposed him from his situation as second officer, and made him change his residence from the cabin to the forecastle.

And where was Mark while these busy scenes were enacted on board the Saladin? He had exulted in the prospect of going on shore, landing on the little island of St. Paul, after having been confined to a ship for several weeks. On reaching the island, and stepping out of the boat on the rock, he was almost beside himself with joy. He shook off the exuberance of his animal spirits by rambling about, and taking the lead in climbing cliffs and precipices, shouting and frolicking, and seeking after novelties, until an hour

7

passed away, and he became fatigued with such violent exercise, with the sun pouring its vertical rays upon his head.

After a while he reached the extreme southern point of the islet, and while examining a wild-looking cavity, discovered the entrance to a grotto, scooped out of the solid rock by the action of the waves, which for ages had been beating and dashing, sometimes with tremendous force, against the island of Ponedo. He passed through the narrow aperture, and entered the cavern. He found the air cool and refreshing, for there the rays of the sun had never penetrated. He seated himself on the fragment of a rock, and leaned back lazily against the wall of the cave, intending to rest for a few minutes, and then make his way back to the boat. But unfortunately he was overtaken by sleep, the kind agent provided by a bountiful Creator to relieve the fatigues and renovate the physical condition of man, and which sometimes makes us forgetful of our interests and recreant to our duties.

Mark Rowland slept in this secluded nook long and soundly, lulled by the murmuring of the waves as they broke on the iron-bound shore. He was at last awakened by a stunning peal of thunder, which reverberated from the walls of the cavern. He sprang to his feet, greatly alarmed, and for a few moments was unconscious of his situation. He rushed to the mouth of the grotto, and listened with dismay to the raging of the wind and the waves, and the pattering of the heavy raindrops against the rocks. The stern reality of his situation then burst upon him, and he realized the terrible evil that had befallen him. In defiance of the tempest, which was then at its height, he left the grotto, and madly hastened, climbing over the rocks in his way, and leaping over dangerous chasms, towards that part of the island on which he had landed in the morning, and where he hoped to find the boat. But to his great embarrassment and grief, the boat was no longer there.

Mark looked around upon the rocks, but not a human being was to be seen. He looked towards the ocean for the Saladin, but the ship shrouded in the mist and rain was no longer visible. He felt now that he was deserted; that he was left on that barren rock in the midst of the ocean, to exist, perhaps, a few days in dreadful solitude, and then die of starvation — a dreadful death! And there, upon a beet-ling crag which overhung the foaming breakers, the poor sailor-boy sat, regardless of the storm which raged around him. And there he long remained, looking out upon the vast watery plain before him, seeking but in vain to pierce the thick veil which concealed the ship from his view.

At length the storm ceased, the clouds rolled away. The rays of the setting sun gilded the cliffs and peaks above him, and the whole extended horizon appeared like a far-off circular line drawn around the island. He then climbed the highest pinnacle of the rocks, and gazed intently in every direction. His forebodings had not deceived him. The ship Saladin had sailed away on her voyage, and Mark Rowland was left on the island of St. Paul.

This was a fearful shock to his feelings. The sudden change in his condition for a time bereft him of all his for-titude, and he was overwhelmed with grief. He thought of his home, of his mother, his brother and sister, those dear ones whom he had left to become a sailor, with the hope and determination to improve their condition, and render their home more comfortable and happy. He thought of the ship, of the kind and indulgent captain, and the friendly and jovial crew, with whom he had been pleasantly associated only a few hours before. And then the desolation of his situation recurred to him, arrayed in the darkest colors. He was alone on the island, without provisions or resources of any description, abandoned by his shipmates, undoubtedly, under the mistaken impression — a very natural one under the circumstances — that some fatal accident had befallen him. Bitterly he reproached himself, and rued his folly in lingering in the cavern, and subjecting himself to such terrible consequences. He knew that the island was but a cluster of barren rocks in the midst of the wide Atlantic, and but rarely seen; and his imagination continued to picture, in fearful·distinctness, a miserable, lingering death.

As the shades of evening advanced, — and they come on rapidly after sunset in those latitudes, — Mark, in a despairing mood, threw himself in a hollow among the rocks, but he could not sleep. For a long time he lay pondering on his unhappy condition, and indulging gloomy conjectures respecting his future fate. Then he arose and looked out upon the wide-spread ocean, upon which darkness, like a funeral pall, seemed to rest. Then he gazed upon the heavens above, again obscured with clouds, hardly a star deigning to send forth its bright beams to cheer his desponding heart. All, everything, seemed to remind him the more forcibly of his solitude, destitution, and helplessness.

But now, as he stood, as it were, on the very verge of despair, his guardian angel. brought to view in bright and living characters, the religious precepts which a good and pious mother had early sought to inculcate on his mind. He dropped on his knees and prayed to God for support and assistance in that dark hour of peril and tribulation. His mind became comparatively calm. He soon fell asleep, and slept soundly several hours.

And while he slept, a change came over his spirits, and he was blessed with pleasant dreams. He dreamed that after having passed through a whole host of wild adventures, he was suddenly transported by some magic influence to his home in the little village of Glenmaple. His mother, with

Albert and Ellen, came forth to meet him, and greeted him with embraces and kisses. They led him into their dwelling, no longer an humble one, dedicated to poverty, but a beautiful, light, and airy edifice, in the centre of a large garden, teeming with fruits and flowers.

To his great surprise and delight, they ushered him into a spacious hall, where the furniture was gay and elegant, and a volume of light, dazzling with its brilliancy, burst upon his vision from a countless number of golden lamps, suspended from the ceiling.

And while he looked upon the scene, bewildered and overjoyed, his mother threw open the folding-doors at the end of the apartment, and a whole bevy of children rushed in, with loud and uproarious shouts of welcome, and surrounded him, halloing and screaming in his very ears their mad delight at his safe return, until he became stunned and stupified with the noise, and begged them to have mercy and desist, but in vain. The lamps burned more painfully brilliant, and the shouts of triumph and welcome became more and more loud, shrill, and discordant, until he awoke and found to his great disappointment that the whole scene, which was stamped on his mind like a beautiful reality, was only a dream!

The brilliant light which flashed upon his eyes was no other than the dazzling rays of the sun, which, as that luminary was now high in the heavens, streamed on his face and awoke him, and the loud and uproarious shouts of welcome from children were changed into the screams of a countless number of sea-birds, which, flying about him, and manifesting their surprise and anger at his presence, soon brought him to his senses.

He rubbed his eyes and crawled out of the cavity in which he had ensconced himself, and looked around. Sleep had

7*

restored his exhausted faculties; his dream had brought comfort, and he no longer indulged in desponding forebodings. Hope, like a benignant angel, came to his assistance, and he resolved to lose no time in taking a full survey of the place on which he had so unexpectedly become a resident, and learn something of its resources and means of sustaining life.

He soon saw enough to convince him that, although his condition was by no means a pleasant one, it was not altogether hopeless. He was alone, it was true. This was a great misfortune. There was no one to converse with, to share in his fears, to sympathize in his hopes, or advise him in regard to his actions. He must rely altogether on himself, and devise means of procuring subsistence on this barren rock, and make himself as comfortable as circumstances would permit, until some passing vessel should discover his forlorn condition and take him off.

He now recalled to mind that he had heard Captain Somers say that the island of St. Paul was seldom fallen in with by ships on the passage to India, or on their return from ports beyond the Cape of Good Hope, and he sighed as he thought that months, perhaps years, might elapse, before any vessel would pass the island near enough to see his signals, and take him on board. And it became an important question how in the meantime he should find means of subsistence? What did the island produce to satisfy his hunger and contribute to his comfort?

Mark walked across the island, and looked around him on every side; but he saw nothing belonging to the vegetable kingdom which was calculated to cheer his spirits and strengthen his hopes. No fruits nor edible roots of any description were to be found. There were birds, however, of the web-footed tribe, in abundance. He could easily capture them if he wished, for they were unaccustomed to the sight of man, and although much disturbed and angry at his presence, were hardly disposed to get out of his way. The eggs of these sea-birds, deposited in rude nests, he found in great profusion among the rocks.

CHAPTER VII.

HERMIT LIFE.

WHILE carefully examining the rocks near the spot where the boat's crew had landed the day before, Mark Rowland found a couple of fishing-lines, with the hooks attached, that had been forgotten by Mr. Smeaton in the hurry of his departure. He rejoiced at this, for he knew that with their aid he would he able to catch fish whenever he took a fancy for such a luxury. He thus ascertained beyond a doubt that he could procure on the island, with hardly any trouble, an abundant supply of eggs, fish, and fowl. But a shade came over his mind when he reflected that, unfortunately, he had no fire by which to cook them.

He had heard that the savages in America procured fire by rubbing together two pieces of dry wood. There were a few sticks and branches of trees and pieces of boards and small spars on the eastern shore of the island, that had been driven high up among the rocks by the action of the winds and the waves. He selected a couple of pieces of wood which he thought would answer his purpose, and rubbed them together for a long time. But although he succeeded in producing by the friction a very sensible heat, he failed to obtain fire, or even to raise a smoke. He often repeated the experiment, but always with a similar unsatisfactory result. It should be mentioned, however, that the wood which he was obliged to use had been, soaking in salt water for weeks or months before it was thrown on the rocks.

Otherwise it is quite probable he would have succeeded in obtaining all the comforts and conveniences which a fire would have furnished, and which are many, even in a tropical climate.

Mark found, greatly to his satisfaction, abundance of fresh water in the hollows of the rocks, which had fallen in the late rains, and fearing that it might evaporate, he prudently took measures immediately to prevent such a result by covering these pools with bushes and boards, and thus screening them, so far as it was in his power, from the tropical heat. And as rain fell in abundance at brief intervals during his stay on the island, he never wanted for pure fresh water — a blessing indeed! for which he was devoutly thankful.

The second day that Mark passed on the island, although he longed for a plentiful meal, he partook of no food excepting some bird's eggs, which he swallowed raw, from necessity rather than choice, and solaced his thirst with water. But on the following day, he was much gratified to find clinging to the rocks, and in the little basins filled with sea-water, shell-fish of various kinds, and among them a species resembling the oyster, which he tasted and found delicious. Here at once he became possessed of an almost inexhaustible supply of nutritious food, and was relieved of all fears of immediate starvation.

He found a cavity in the rocks, overhung by a frowning cliff. He took possession of it, and with little trouble converted it into an eligible sleeping-chamber. By covering the bottom with coarse grass and dried gulf-weed, which he could procure in any quantity, he made a soft and luxurious bed, on which he threw himself whenever he sought repose, by night or by day, and buried his cares, his griefs, and his hopes, in sleep.

On a huge cliff which jutted into the ocean on the northern part of the island, he contrived to erect the tallest pole or spar which he could find, as a flag-staff, on the top of which, by means of one of his fishing-lines, he could at any moment display, as a signal of distress, the thin nankeen jacket which he fortunately wore when he left the ship with a light and joyous heart, exulting in the prospect of exploring a desert island.

At the foot of this flag-staff, from which he could survey the whole line of the horizon, he often passed his evening hours, refreshed by the cool breezes, after suffering from the stifling heat of the day ; and every morning before the rising of the sun he sought this cliff, and threw around a searching gaze, hoping to see some friendly vessel which would take him from his solitary abode and return him to his friends.

When Mark had been about a week the sole human inhabitant of the island of St. Paul he was surprised one morning on visiting a low point near the water's edge, to find that the salt water which had filled some of the hollows of the rocks, had evaporated, owing to the extreme heat of the sun for several days, and left crystals of salt. He tasted it and satisfied himself that there was no mistake in the matter. It was genuine salt, and he now recollected to have heard that a large portion of the salt used was made by the evaporation of salt water. He was delighted at this discovery, for he had deeply felt the want of this condiment, which is so necessary in the preparation and preservation of food. He went busily to work, and collected a good supply, lest he might not meet with such another opportunity, and deposited it in a nook where it would not be exposed to the action of the rains.

Before he made this discovery, he had at various times caught fish with the lines left behind by the sailors ; but he found it an exceedingly difficult matter to eat them raw, without salt or seasoning of any description. He now again caught some fish, split them open, and sprinkled them with salt as he had seen his mother do with the pickerel he sometimes caught in Rhadamanthus pond. He then placed them in the sun, which dried them, when they could be kept for' months, and proved a very acceptable species of food. Thus Mark found, that by a little skill, address, and calculation, he was in little danger of being a great sufferer from hunger or thirst, for a long while to come.

The kinds of food were not such as he had been accustomed to, or such as he would have chosen if a variety had been set before him, and they would have been wonderfully improved if they had gone through the process of cooking. But he had no choice, and devoured with a good appetite such viands as by enterprise and ingenuity he was able to procure. What he most felt the need of was bread, or some substitute, as potatoes ; but he knew that nothing of the kind could be obtained, and, like a true philosopher, avoided pining after luxuries, and made up his mind to make the best of his condition without them.

Mark had been on the island about a month, when one day he was busily engaged in pulling up some coarse grass, which was rooted in the soil of bird-lime or guano that abounded in some of the cavities. With this grass he had been for some days exerting all his ingenuity in an attempt to manufacture an apology for a hat. On raising his head and looking abroad, his joy and astonishment may be conceived, when he saw a vessel, a large brig, but a few miles off, standing to the southward, under a press of sail, urged on her way by a pleasant breeze from the eastward.

His heart throbbed with excitement. His exile was surely ended ! He would soon be among his fellow-creatures once more, gay and happy ! He hastened to the flag-staff on the cliff and hoisted his jacket, and fearing that it might not be large enough to be distinctly seen at a distance, stripped himself of his shirt, in order to magnify his signal.

But the grief and disappointment of Mark may be imagined, when the brig after having reached the position nearest to the island in passing, continued on her course and made no sign! Mark's signal was disregarded, and, being but a few feet above the rock, was in all probability unseen; for it is difficult to suppose that any man could see a signal of distress flying from a desert island, without heaving-to at once, and daring all risks in dispatching a boat to learn its meaning.

A few weeks after this incident, while Mark was engaged in searching among the rocks on the sea-shore for a species of shell-fish which he found by experience to be delicious food, he saw in a little hollow, just out of reach of the breakers, what appeared to be a piece of leather, half buried beneath the gravel. Surprised at such an unwonted sight, he took hold of it in order to ascertain its character and condition. He pulled and tugged with all his force to get it from the place where it had been thrown by chance, cr hidden designedly, and, to his great astonishment, he drew forth a bag, containing something not bulky, but extremely heavy. The string which confined the mouth of the bag was decayed, and fell apart while he was extricating the bag from the gravel, and his exultation and joy knew no bounds when he found that the leathern bag was filled with golden coins! He had discovered a treasure on the desert island.

But his exultation at the sight of gold was not of long duration. His reason soon convinced him that these golden coins were of no use to him in his present condition. And as he saw no immediate prospect of leaving the island, and longed for a change of food, he would gladly have exchanged the whole pile of doubloons for a few loaves of bread, or a dozen of baked potatoes.

How the bag of money, which was as heavy as he could convenicntly carry, became deposited in that desolate spot, was a problem that never was solved. He supposed it must have belonged to some unfortunate men who were cast away on the island with their treasure, and died of grief and hunger. And he shuddered as he thought that their unhappy fate might eventually be his own. His conjectures were confirmed on discovering in a cavity among the rocks, in the neighborhood of the spot where he found the gold, some bones, bleached by the sun and rain, which he felt assured were a part of a human skeleton. This frightful discovery put a stop to further investigations in that quarter of the island.

One moonlight evening Mark climbed to the summit of the cliff to enjoy the sea-breeze, at the close of a very sultry day, as he was wont to do. He seated himself on a rock, his back resting against the flag-staff, and looked abroad upon the ocean. His spirits were unusually depressed, for he was sick of solitude, and had been thinking of his home. For more than two hours he remained watching the rippling of the waves and the dancing of the moonbeams. Mark did not altogether despond, but he was beginning to grow impatient at his long stay on the island. It was strongly impressed on his mind that it would not be his fate to be left there to die miserably, alone, and by inches; but that, sooner or later, he would be rescued by some passing ship.

And this confidence in his future good fortune, this unshaken belief that "better days were coming," did noble service in sustaining his health amid the deprivations and troubles which surrounded him, and which would have crushed to the earth never to rise again, the spirits and frame of one who cherished no hope, but abandoned himself to despair. And Mark was right. He reasoned according to the dictates of sound philosophy. We can hardly conceive of a situation

8

in life so deplorable as to be altogether hopeless, where by the energetic exercise of the gifts we have received from our Creator, there is no possibility of escaping an impending danger, or improving our condition, however depressed or however perilous.

While Mark was gazing vacantly on the broad sheet spread out before him, and listening to the hoarse and irregular sound of the breakers as they dashed against the rocks, and recalling the past, sighing over the present, and speculating on the future, he was roused from his reveries by the sight of a white speck on the distant horizon, the line of which in the clear, cloudless night was distinctly defined. The moon by this time was nearly on the meridian. Could this white speck be the moon's pure rays reflected from the sails of a ship? It must be so; there could be no other mode of explaining the unusual phenomenon.

Mark was deeply agitated; the dim appearance of a vessel afar off, filled his mind with associations and hopes of the most buoyant tendency. A vessel was in sight, bearing on its decks human beings. His solitude, which was becoming unbearable, seemed already relieved of half its weight.

The speck became rapidly enlarged. It was soon manifest that the vessel, with a large spread of canvas, was approaching under a fine breeze, and steering a straight course for the island. He kept his eye on that vessel, and with intense interest watched her proceedings. And now he longed for the means of making a fire on the rock, a beacon-light to warn mariners of their danger, and notify them that a wretched being was chained to that desolate spot, and doomed to perish miserably, unless some assistance was speedily tendered.

As the vessel drew near, her course continued unchanged. She steered directly for the island, being apparently close-hauled on the wind. The moon shone out with unusual splendor, and he could see the sails, and even the hull of a large ship, as plainly as if it were midday.

Mark's joy was changed to anxiety for the fate of that vessel. Were those on board aware that they were near the land? Had they no suspicion of danger? Where was the lookout? Where the officer of the deck? Were they all wrapped in sleep, and the ship left to its own guidance and that of a sleepy helmsman?

The ship came onward, plunging through the water. He could see the snow-white foam beneath her bows. But not a man was visible on deck. In a few minutes, unless her course was altered, that noble vessel would be wrecked on the rocks which lined that part of the island of St. Paul.

At that moment the selfish idea flitted across his mind, that if the ship struck the rocks and went to pieces, his own condition in all likelihood would be greatly improved. He would thus gain some companions; perhaps food, fire, and clothing; also, perhaps, boats, materials for a tent, and many comforts and necessaries, the absence of which had caused him much inconvenience and suffering: and also ultimately the means of leaving the island and returning to his native land.

But the mind of Mark Rowland was too noble to harbor such selfish reflections. They were dismissed almost before they attained a definite shape. He felt instinctively that they were wrong; that it was his duty — a duty from which he could not shrink without feeling himself a craven and a criminal — to exert every means in his power to warn the careless crew of that ship of their danger, that they might steer clear of the rocks and proceed on their voyage in safety.

Acting upon this generous impulse, as soon as the ship, dashing onward towards destruction, drew near enough to the rock to make it likely that his voice could be heard, he began to hail in a loud and shrill voice, " Ship ahoy! ship ahoy! Hard-up your helm, or you will be ashore! Port! Hard-a-port! Ship ahoy-oy-oy! Hard-a-port your helm!"

The warning voice of Mark Rowland was heard, probably, by the helmsman, nodding at his post; and the sleepy crew and officers were aroused. There was a great commotion on deck, and a running to and fro of the men. Orders were given and repeated, and the shouting and swearing were on a large scale. In the midst of the tumult, the helm was undoubtedly changed, for the ship fell off from the wind, just grazed the rocks, and passing so near that Mark could have tossed a pebble on board, rapidly proceeded on her course. The loud and imploring entreaties of Mark that a boat might be sent ashore to take him off, were probably not heard in the confusion, or if heard were unheeded, for the ship's way continued unchecked and she soon disappeared in the southwest.

Mark's disappointment was great. He had heard the voices of his fellow-men, and he yearned to be with them again. It was long that night before he closed his eyes in sleep; and the next morning, when he awoke, the scene so exciting, so unsatisfactory, and so short-lived, seemed like a feverish dream.

Days, weeks, and months passed away, — how many, Mark knew not, for he kept no record of time. Although he was untiring in keeping a vigilant lookout, only one vessel was seen by him during this long, tedious period. This was a ship from the southward, with a fair wind and plenty of it, which went dashing along, homeward bound, thought Mark, with royals, skysails and studding-sails set; and passing within a couple of leagues, took no notice of the signal which Mark displayed from the summit of the cliff.

And now Mark experienced a trouble which he had not calculated upon. His diet, although not unpalatable, was not favorable to health. His strength failed, his activity was diminished, and his frame became emaciated; and it is no wonder that, notwithstanding his constitutional courage and fortitude, he became at times dejected and unhappy. He thought that if he had one companion, whatever might be his race, color, age, habits, or disposition, with whom he could converse and advise and sympathize, it would relieve the monotony of his condition and contribute to his happiness. He envied Robinson Crusoe the companionship of Friday, and proved in his own case the truth of the old proverb, "misery loves company."

He finally hit upon an expedient to procure some companions, some living creatures to whom he could become attached, and which would love him in return. He tamed a couple of young sea-gulls, which he named Albert and Ellen, the names of his brother and sister. After a large expenditure of patience and perseverance, he succeeded in educating them according to his wishes. They would hop around him, accompany him in his excursions, enjoy his caresses, and perch on his shoulders. He passed some hours every day in fondling and playing with his pets.

Mark found considerable exercise in scrambling about among the rocks; but as he could not always be doing this or playing with his sea-gulls, which proved to be more stupid than intelligent, he felt the need of some pleasant occupation or amusement to divert his mind from the contemplation of his troubles. He was fond of swimming, and the smooth sea under the lee of the islet often tempted him to plunge in and enjoy the grateful exercise at the close of a sultry day, or in the morning, while the sun was emerging from his watery bed.

But he denied himself this indulgence, for fear of meeting some "companions of the bath," of whom he had a wholesome dread. More than once he had seen enough to con-

8*

vince him that the waters which washed the shores of St,
Paul were inhabited by sharks of uncommon size and ferocity. He knew, from experience, that the monsters took a
natural liking to him, and would gladly welcome him to their
native element, and give him painful but decided proofs of
their attachment to his person. But their affection was not
reciprocated, and Mark wisely determined to give them a
wide berth as long as it was in his power. .

But there was a pool in the south side of the island, some
eight or ten fathoms in diameter, and of unknown depth,
which communicated with the ocean by means of a short
canal or chasm in the rock, where the water was not more
than six or eight feet deep. He longed to bathe in this pool
when he first examined it, but put a curb on his longings
when he saw that a large shark, a shovel-nosed shark, had
possession; and he felt no disposition to dispute the man-
eating rascal's title to the sovereignty. Several times afterwards he saw one or more of these grim-looking gentlemen,
swimming slowly about near the surface, and for a time he
left them to the undisputed enjoyment of all the pleasures
of the pool.

Nevertheless, Mark thought it hard that he should thus
be deprived of the pleasure of bathing in that hot climate,
and after a while devised a plan to keep out the sharks, and
monopolize the pool. Fragments of rock abounded in that
part of the island, and he went vigorously at work to fill the
canal with rocks of large size, disposed in such a way that,
without preventing the flow of water, they would serve as an
effectual barrier to the merciless tyrants.

This was a laborious task, and occupied a large portion of
his time for two or three weeks. But he finally completed
the work, greatly to his own satisfaction, and exulted in having ousted the original possessors of the pool, and converted
it into a bathing-place for his own especial use. Hardly a

day passed that he did not spend an hour at least in the
water, swimming and diving and practising other submarine
feats, until he became almost amphibious.

One day as Mark was fishing for a species of large red
fish, which as an article of food he preferred to any of the
finny tribe, he felt a decided bite. He pulled, but could not
start the fish: Soon the fish pulled in his turn, and was very
near dragging Mark from the shelving crag into the water.
He took a turn with his line around the corner of a rock,
soon after which the fish rose to the surface, and to the great
disgust of our youthful fisherman, proved to be a shark.
As soon as he came in sight, he made a short but decisive
struggle, broke the fishing-gear, and swam leisurely away,
feloniously carrying off the two hooks and a couple of fathoms of line, and, as it appeared to Mark, shaking his tail in
derision.

Mark was justly indignant at such atrocious conduct, and
resolved from that moment to make war, and war to the
knife, upon that man-tormenting and man-eating race, which
seemed to be always interfering with his comfort or threatening his life. He determined henceforth to make it a pleasure, a recreation, a business, to annoy, and, if possible, destroy, every shark which dared approach the rocks that lined
the island of St. Paul.

This was a lucky idea, so far as he was concerned, although
it was neither pleasant nor profitable to the sharks. It furnished him with occupation and amusement, and prevented
him from dwelling on his misfortunes, and lamenting his
protracted stay on that desert island. He really enjoyed
the sport, as he called it; and followed it up with the energy
which was a distinguishing trait in his character.

He would tie to the end of his fishing-line a tempting morsel, in the shape of a sea-fowl stripped of its feathers and
split open, and throw it as far from the rocks as his strength

would allow, and then slowly draw it towards him. In this way, if there were any sharks in the vicinity, he would toll them around, and lure them in closely under the rocks. Then, taking advantage of his commanding position, he would punch them with a heavy pole, sharpened at one end, which made them exceedingly uncomfortable and angry, or throw down upon their heads huge pieces of rock, as heavy as he could lift, which would seriously unsettle their understandings, and, in some cases, when the work was skilfully done, destroy life.

On one occasion he narrowly escaped becoming a victim to his destructive zeal. He had succeeded, after having for hours exerted all his skill, in enticing within reach of his missiles, a shark of the largest size, and secretly determined to punish him severely for the trouble he had caused him. For this purpose he selected a large piece of angular rock, and raised it as high as he could reach, directly over his unsuspecting foe, and then using the warning language which he had often heard on shipboard, he called out, " Stand from under ! " and brought down the heavy missile, propelling it with all his force upon the monster's head.

Unfortunately, Mark was so much interested in his attempt to destroy the shark, that he neglected to take care of himself. As the stone left his hands, his foot slipped, he lost his balance, and, following the stone, found himself, to his surprise and terror, the next moment sitting astride on the back of the shark. The animal, frightened at such an unexpected visitation, and probably severely injured by the falling stone, suddenly sunk down in the water, and sheered off to a distance, and Mark saw him no more.

Mark was greatly alarmed at this unlooked-for change in his position. He knew not that other sharks were not lying in wait to be revenged on the hated persecutor of their race, and exerted all his strength and skill in swimming to a spot some twenty yards off, where he could crawl out of the water on to the rocks, fearing and more than half suspecting, at every stroke he took, that a shark was at his heels in full chase, and would soon fasten on one of his limbs.

This incident taught Mark Rowland a useful lesson, and ever afterwards, whenever he set a steel trap for an enemy, he took especial pains to avoid putting his own foot in it.

CHAPTER VIII.

OCEAN DEITIES!

ONE morning, as Mark was standing on the rocks by the margin of the pool, and, preparing for a swim, had thrown off the ragged garments which constituted his whole wardrobe, and was about to take the refreshing plunge, he beheld, greatly to his astonishment, a strange-looking head pop up out of the water but a few fathoms from the shore. The head somewhat resembled the head of a dog, and yet the features, taken together, had a sort of human look, reminding one of an exceedingly homely, repulsive-looking savage, with hairy face and neck, and bright sparkling eyes.

This creature fixed his eyes steadily on Mark, as if to inquire who he was, and what business he had on the island. Before Mark could recover from his surprise at the sight of such an unexpected intruder, another head of a similar stamp showed itself near the same spot, and with a defiant expression, indicating that he was not to be trifled with, also looked hard at the cabin-boy.

Mark remained motionless, and in turn stared hard at these inquisitive animals. Both parties were puzzled. What they thought of Mark, as he stood there on the rocks, with uncombed hair, bronzed features, and naked limbs, was never recorded. Mark had heard of sea-serpents and mermaids, sea-lions and seals, walrusses and krakens, and other monsters which are said to inhabit the great deep, and sometimes show themselves to highly-favored mariners. Whether the animals with these strange-looking heads, and who appeared to feel themselves perfectly at home, belonged to either of those tribes, was more than his learning or sagacity could declare.

In a few minutes the heads, as if satisfied with their scrutiny, and believing they had nothing to fear from the strange and awkward-looking figure on the rocks, disappeared. Mark was indignant at this invasion of his dominions, and was particularly incensed at the idea of their taking possession of his "pool" for the performance of their ablutions. These interlopers had a saucy and dangerous look. He did not like their appearance, and felt unwilling to enter the waters which they inhabited. He waited a while on the rocks to see if they would show themselves again. But as they chose to remain invisible to him, he resumed his tattered garments, and slowly walked away.

A few mornings afterwards, Mark saw an animal of a clumsy, uncouth shape, covered with hair, with a head similar to the ones he had seen so unexpectedly thrust out of the water, and legs and arms, somewhat resembling the fins of a fish, stretched out lazily on a rock, close to the edge of the pool. As Mark went towards it and hallooed, the creature slipped off the rock into the water, and he saw him no more.

Mark felt a desire to learn something more of the nature and habits of his new visitors, and determined to watch their haunts and study their characters, and, if desirable, cultivate their acquaintance. In all likelihood he would have carried his project into effect, and established a treaty of friendship with these intruders, had not an incident occurred which entirely changed the position of his affairs, and rendered such a scheme impracticable.

He had been on the bleak and barren island of St. Paul

about eight months, when early one morning, attended by his pets, the sea-gulls, he mounted the high cliff on which he had erected his flagstaff. He looked abroad to see if any vessel was in the offing; but he had been so often disappointed, that he did this more through habit than with the expectation of seeing a ship approaching the island. As he looked towards the north-west, he fancied he saw a dark spot afar off. He rubbed his eyes and looked again. It was no deceptive vision. The object, whatever it might be, was still there. It was not long before, to his great delight, he made it out to be a ship, for the sun had now risen, and he could distinguish the sails.

The ship appeared to increase in size, and her outlines became every moment more distinct, a convincing proof that she was coming towards the island. With great glee Mark fastened his old jacket to the top of the flag-pole as a signal of distress. Then seated himself on the rock, with his birds resting on his shoulders, and awaited, with mingled expectation, anxiety, and joy, the result.

The breeze was moderate, and the ship slowly approached, but gave no indications of changing her course. If she kept on, she would pass the island within less than a league, and at that distance not only the signal, but the flagstaff, and even Mark himself, could be seen from the decks without a spy-glass.

Mark felt that the crisis of his fate was at hand; that if this ship passed by without noticing his signal, as others had done, he could no longer cherish any hope, and that *his* skeleton would soon be bleaching on the rocks.

But Mark was not doomed to suffer again the pangs of disappointment, and his suspense was not of great duration; for, long before he supposed the stranger was near enough to make out his signal, he beheld, to his inexpressible delight, the broad American ensign leave the quarter-deck of the ship, and after fluttering a moment in the air, wave gracefully from the spanker peak.

His signal was seen. His signal was answered. He knew that in a few hours, at most, he would escape from his long imprisonment on a desert island, and again enjoy the blessings of social intercourse with friends and countrymen. With heartfelt gratitude he dropped on his knees, and offered his fervent thanks to the Almighty.

The ship which Mark saw was the Rosamond, of·Boston, bound from New York to the Cape of Good Hope. The captain, whose name was Lamark, was a thorough seaman, a skilful navigator, and an honest man. He knew that a current had set him to the westward, and that he must be near the meridian of St Paul. The wind having hauled far to the north, he was steering a south-east course, and had ordered a good lookout to be kept as the ship drew near the latitude of the island; and just as the sun was making its appearance in the east, the craggy rocks of St. Paul were plainly seen from the foretop-mast head.

As there were no dangerous rocks or shoals in the vicinity, and as the island lay directly in his course, Captain Lamark determined to pass as near to it as he could do with safety, for the purpose of gratifying his curiosity. As the ship approached the land, the captain was surprised to see with his spy-glass a pole on the highest point, with a flag flying. He divined the meaning of the signal at once; he knew that there must be some poor shipwrecked sailors on that desolate spot, and he ordered the American ensign to be hoisted immediately, to assure them that help was at hand, and the quarter-boat to be got in readiness for an expedition to the shore. The Rosamond passed along the eastern or windward side of the island, and when about a mile off, the ship was hove-to, the boat was lowered, and Captain Lamark ordered Mr. Hawkins, the second officer, to go to the lee-

9

side of the island, land there if it were possible, and bring off any person or persons whom he might find there in distress.

As Mr. Hawkins approached the shore, he was greeted with shouts of welcome by the half-naked, pale, and emaciated Mark Rowland, who hastened to the water's edge, almost crazy with joy. Mr. Hawkins landed with some difficulty, and after asking a few questions of the wild and half-starved looking being, the only human inhabitant of the island, and after giving his hand a hearty grip to assure him of his protection, ordered the men to gather some eggs, which were abundant in that neighborhood, while he assisted Mark in placing his prize, the bag of golden coins, in the boat. Mark then jumped in, accompanied by his interesting companions of long standing ; the sailors followed, and in a few minutes the deserted cabin-boy and his treasure and his darling friends, the birds, were safe on board the good ship Rosamond. Orders were given to " fill away," and the ship dashed merrily along towards her destined port.

Mark was received in the kindest manner by Captain Lamark, who welcomed him on board the Rosamond, listened to his story with much interest, and promised to take good care of him and his treasure. He took him into the cabin, and caused a good meal to be placed before him, to which Mark did ample justice. He supplied Mark with clothes from his own trunk, which, although much too large for him in his present condition, after a few reefs had been taken in them, answered the purpose passably well. He furnished Mark with a berth, or sleeping-place, in the steerage, and learned from his lips the particulars of his short, but humble and eventful life.

When Mark had concluded his narrative, the worthy captain again shook his hand, and told him his troubles were over, that the ship Rosamond was bound to the Cape of

Good Hope, and back to a port in the United States, probably to Boston, and that if he did not fall in with a ship from
the East India seas, bound home, to which vessel Mark could
be transferred, if he wished, he might safely calculate to be
landed in Boston in four months or four months and a half,
at farthest, and could then start off without a moment's delay to his home, where his presence would shed plenty and
joy over his mother's hearth. "And I will pledge my word,"
said Captain Lamark, with emphasis, "that you shall not
again be left on a desert island, to subsist for months on
raw eggs and scallops, taming sea-gulls, tormenting sharks,
and hunting for hidden treasures."

Mark slept soundly the night following his rescue from
the island, and, accustomed to early rising, was on deck
soon after sunrise, enjoying through every nerve and fibre
of his frame, his changed condition. He found Captain
Lamark on deck, talking earnestly with the first officer, Mr.
Digges. He learned from their conversation that the ship,
having run about sixty miles since leaving St. Paul, was
now on the equator, and that the time-hallowed custom of
shaving those who had never crossed the line, and introduc-
ing them to Old Neptune and his wife, was to be observed
on board the Rosamond.

Mark had heard the crew of the Saladin discuss this subject, and his curiosity was excited; and being assured that,
in consequence of his delicate health and long residence
within a degree of the equator, Old Neptune would have
little or nothing to say to him; he rejoiced that the mystic
ceremonies were going to take place, and manifested much
interest in the proceedings, which proved to be a regular
frolic, and a series of practical and coarse jokes at the expense of the poor fellows who had never been south of the
equator.

Immediately after breakfast, Mr. Hawkins, the second

mate, a regular case-hardened old sailor, who had followed the sea for thirty years, and had never risen to the dignity of first officer, went aloft, and was soon heard to hail, " On deck there ! "

" Hallo ! " responded the captain ; " what's adrift now ? "

" I see a sail-boat, sir, a long way off, steering directly for the ship ! "

" Ah ! " exclaimed Captain Lamark, " I thought it was about time. That must be Old Neptune ! How many are there in the boat ? "

" Three persons, as well as I can make out."

" Aye," said the skipper, " Old Neptune and his wife, and the barber ! Come down, Mr. Hawkins, we must prepare to receive them with all due honor and respect."

Among the ship's company, consisting of fifteen persons, it was found on investigation that three had never crossed the equinoctial line, and were of course entitled to the particular attentions of Old Neptune. These three unfortunate men were sent by Mr. Hawkins into the half-deck, when the hatch-way was closed, and they were imprisoned until preparations were made for their introduction to the Monarch of the Seas.

It was determined that Mr Hawkins should personate Neptune. He was to appear in full costume. His grim features were made to look more grim, by liberal dashes of the paint-brush, dipped in blue, red, and white colors. His head was covered by a huge mass of gulf-weed, ingeniously arranged to represent a crown, although, as it hung down in festoons about his ears and neck, it bore a nearer resemblance to an enormous wig. His chest and brawny arms were bare, but covered with blotches of paint of diverse hues. His only garment was a tunic, hastily manufactured for the occasion out of the ship's private signal, a square flag, half blue and half red. A slit was cut in the centre, the head was thrust through, and the garment, in the style of a *poncho*, was complete. In one hand he held a short speaking-trumpet; in the other a three-pronged grainse; and assuming a majestic attitude, made a truly imposing appearance, and was believed by his shipmates to be a capital likeness of the Ocean King.

His wife Amphitrite was personated by a jolly little tar, named Archie Stobbs. His face was also painted, but in a style intended to give him a gentle and feminine appearance, which was done by painting his cheeks and the tip of his nose of a lively red, his eyebrows black, and the rest of his face a clear white. A small, delicate moustache, created by drawing the black paint-brush across the upper lip, added to the piquancy and character of the features. His head was profusely decked with gulf-weed, ingeniously twisted into curls and ringlets, which fell gracefully upon the shoulders, and, reaching to the waist, were met by a nondescript garment, considered appropriate for the occasion, and made out of a calico counterpane which rejoiced in all the colors of the rainbow, and was indeed a great curiosity, belonging to Captain Lamark, and a present from his grandmother. Clad in this costume, little Archie looked and strutted every inch a queen.

The barber who attended on their majesties was also quaintly arrayed. He held in one hand a tar-bucket, half-filled with the odoriferous fluid diluted with oil, and a tar-brush. In the other he flourished his razor in the guise of a piece of iron hoop, with notches at intervals, to produce a more decided effect.

While these principal actors in the drama about to be performed were getting ready to enter on the scene, the remainder of the crew, under the direction of Mr. Digges, were engaged in drawing water and pouring it into the long-boat; and on the bow of the boat a platform was erected as a throne for the Ocean Deities.

When the arrangements were completed, which occupied fully an hour, the three men, who, in a state of unpleasant suspense, were confined in the half-deck, listened with much interest to the following dialogue, intended for their ears, carried on with speaking trumpets between old Neptune, who was on the bowsprit, and Captain Lamark, standing on the quarter-deck.

"Ship ahoy!"

"Hallo!"

"Where are you from!"

"New York."

"Where bound?"

"Cape of Good Hope."

"Have you any strangers on board?"

"Ay, ay! three fine fellows, who are longing to pay their respects to you."

"All right!" said old Neptune. "I'll step over the gang-way and shave them directly."

In a few minutes the hatchway was opened, and the prisoners were gravely told that Neptune was on board, and one of their number must come on deck and be introduced to him and his wife.

Harry Linsay, a lively young fellow, who had been only one voyage to sea, and was eager to be first on the list, that he might enjoy the subsequent sport, was carefully blindfolded, and led on deck. He was made to ascend to the gunwale of the long-boat by the help of the gangway ladder, and then seated on a plank, fronting their majesties, with his feet and legs immersed in water.

Neptune asked the new proselyte various questions, in a thundering voice through his speaking-trumpet, in relation to his birthplace, age, habits, &c., the answers to which were to be placed on record. He then ordered the barber to do his duty. The lower part of the poor fellow's face and his chin were soon thickly covered with the unsavory lather; and while the operations were going on, sundry questions were asked by the inquisitive potentate, and when his mouth was opened to reply, the waggish barber popped in the tar-brush, to Linsay's great annoyance and disgust. The razor was drawn over his chin in a very careless manner, and the process of being shaved was completed. And now some of the crew who were standing round with buckets and pots full of salt water, poured it upon his devoted head, or dashed it in his face as a purifying rite.

But the bandage was not yet taken off. Old Neptune continued to ask Linsay a number of questions, and the questions and replies were of a nature to elicit shouts of laughter from the sailors. A speaking-trumpet was given him through which to make his responses, under pretense that the king was hard of hearing, and he was also instructed to open his mouth wide and halloo with all his might. But his mouth was no sooner stretched to its utmost capacity, than a bucket of salt water was emptied into the mouth of the trumpet, which conducted it down his throat, almost suffo-cating the unfortunate tyro, while the mirth of the lookers-on waxed fast and furious.

Linsay was then required by Old Neptune to promise on his sacred honor that he would never eat hard bread when he could get soft, unless he liked hard bread best; that he would never go on foot when he could ride, unless he pre-ferred to walk; that he would never stay on shore when he could go to sea, unless he liked land better than water; and that he would kill a shark whenever he could meet one, unless the shark killed him first.

Linsay having complied with these requisitions, Old Neptune cried out in a tone of authority, "Give him the finish-ing touch!"

The plank on which he was seated was instantly knocked

away, and he tumbled heels over head into the water, uttering
a scream, under the impression that he was overboard. At
this moment the bandage which covered his eyes was twitched
off, and he recovered the full use of his senses and his legs,
and looking up saw Old Neptune seated on his throne, with
his wife beside him, holding their sides while indulging in
peals of undignified laughter, and the rest of his shipmates
standing around, heartily joined in the chorus.

The same ceremonies were observed in the case of the
other individuals who had never crossed the line. The frolic
lasted for some hours, when Neptune laid aside his emblems
of authority, and order and discipline, which had been for the
time not a little relaxed, again reigned on board the Rosamond.

Such scenes occasionally tend to break the monotony
which always prevails on shipboard during the long passage
across the tropics and around the Cape of Good Hope or
Cape Horn, and if judiciously managed produce a good effect
on the spirits of the crew. But care should be taken that
the authority of the officers, and the strength of the " one
man power," which is absolutely necessary in sailing a ship,
are not weakened thereby. It should also be recollected that
although it may be sport to those who have already crossed
the equator, it is no sport to those who are subjected to such
humiliation, insult, and sometimes abuse.

CHAPTER IX.

CATCHING A MERMAID.

On the evening after the ship Rosamond crossed the equinoctial line, there was an animated conversation among the ship's company connected with the subjects of the day.

"Old Neptune's idea of shaving a new-comer, and sousing him in salt water afterwards," said little Bob Randy, "is a good one, and makes fun for all hands. It used to be managed more roughly before sailors became civilized, and woe to the man who refused to submit to the whims of Old Neptune. Indeed, I have heard old sailors say that in some ships *keel-hauling* was resorted to when a fellow was foolishly obstinate, and refused to 'come and be shaved,' when about to cross for the first time in his life the equinoctial line."

"Keel-hauling? What's that?" exclaimed Harry Linsay.

"Oh, a very simple operation to take the kinks out of a fellow," replied Bob Randy. "It consists in merely making fast the bight of a rope to a man's body just under the armpits, and passing it under the ship's bottom to the other side of the deck. Then toss him overboard, lowering him gradually with one part of the rope, while half a dozen men, more or less, bowse away at the other. He is thus *hauled beneath the keel* from one side of the ship to the other; and by the time he is roused on deck, he withdraws all objections to being shaved, is docile as a flounder, and obeys orders without grumbling."

"I should think so!" remarked Harry Linsay, with a shudder.

"But the work must be done at once, and with a will," continued Bob Randy, "or I would not give a rope-yarn for the man's life. Suppose he should get foul of the keel, and stick there for a while? That might prove a left-handed joke."

"True as a book, Bob," exclaimed Jack Radkin, a smoke-dried old salt, who had served for years on board an English man-of-war, and was strongly suspected of being a subject of John Bull, notwithstanding his American protection. "But he must take his chance; and if he does not sprawl about while under the ship's bottom, and is careful to keep his legs and arms snug and quiet, he will suffer but little inconvenience. To make all safe, however, it would be well to fasten a twelve-pound shot to his feet, which will sink him clear of the keel, and then the work can be done shipshape, and finished off in a jiffey."

"You speak as if you were an old hand at the business," said Bob Randy. "How is it, Jack?"

"I saw a miserable scoundrel keel-hauled once," said Jack, "and was obliged to lend a hand, and a bungling piece of work we made of it. I could do the job better now; but hope I shall never be called on to test my skill."

"Amen to that, with all my heart!" said Bob. "But how happened you to be inveigled into such a scrape?"

"Oh, it happened when I was a boy, more than twenty-five years ago, before I left the old country. I was an apprentice on board the barque Marlborough, of Bristol, Captain Rockstone, on a voyage from Bristol to Barbadoes. The captain was a kind-hearted, indulgent man, and was greatly liked by the sailors. On the passage home, the steward, who was a Lascar from Calcutta, was shamefully neglectful of his duties, and when reminded of it by the captain, used insolent and mutinous language, for which Captain Rockstone gently touched him up with a rope's end. The fellow swore revenge, and kept his oath.

"On the following night, while the captain was sleeping in his state-room, and Mr. Bolan, the first mate, was attending to his duties on deck, the steward stealthily approached the captain's berth, and with a carving-knife stabbed him to the heart. The unfortunate man could only cry out, ' Help, help! Mr. Stanchell! The villain has murdered me!' when he breathed his last.

" Mr. Stanchell, the second mate, hearing the cry, leaped from his berth, and grappled with the steward, who, dealing him a severe wound with the same weapon, escaped on deck. But the hue and cry was raised, and in less than a minute every man on board knew that the captain was murdered by the steward! The assassin was seized, and by order of the chief mate, who now assumed command of the ship, manacled, and lashed firmly to an eyebolt in the half-deck.

" A consultation, a sort of council of war, was now held on the forecastle by the men, who loved the captain, hated the assassin, and were greatly shocked at the bloody act. After a short discussion, it was agreed to by all hands, that the steward had broken the laws of God and man, had committed a murder, and deserved severe punishment, and as the laws on land were slow in their operation and uncertain, it was our duty to take the matter into our own hands, and make sure that he got his deserts.

" Then the question arose, how should we punish him? One was in favor of hanging him at the yard-arm ; another thought we should strip off his shirt, tie him to the main-rigging, and flog him with a two-inch rope until he could neither speak nor wink ; while more than one thought the best course would be to fasten the grindstone to his neck, and throw him overboard. There was quite a difference of opinion on the sub-

ject, until one of the men suggested *keel-hauling* as a punishment just suited to the crime. The suggestion was
received with universal favor, and it was decided, as with
one voice, that keel-hauling it should be.

" Preparations were immediately made for carrying out the
sentence. Mr. Bolan, the chief mate, was at that moment
below, looking after the comfort of Mr. Stanchell, who had
been badly cut with the assassin's knife. The doors of the
companion-way were closed, and the cabin skylight put on
and secured, to prevent the mate from coming on deck and
being a witness to the scene about to be acted. And for a
similar reason the cook was confined in the forecastle by
fastening the forescuttle. We now had a clear deck; the ship
was hove-to, the lashings which confined the murderer to the
half-deck were cut, and he was hauled up the ladder and
brought forward to the waist. When told of the punishment
in store for him, he was dreadfully agitated, and begged for
mercy. He soon found that that was out of the question,
and entreated to be killed on the spot, a favor which was not
granted.

" The rope was passed under the ship's bottom, and fastened around his body, and, in spite of his struggles and prayers
for mercy, he was thrown overboard to windward. Two of the
sailors were appointed to ' ease him away handsomely,' and
all the others were required to lay hold of the rope which was
to drag him under the keel, and up the ship's side to leeward.
It happened, unfortunately for the steward, that we pulled
too hard, or the others did not lower away fast enough, for
the rascal scraped the ship's bottom, and caused a long
delay by sticking to the keel. After jerking the rope, then
slacking it, and trying various experiments, we got him clear,
and hauled him in on deck in triumph. We had succeeded in
keel-hauling him, but he was dead when we landed him on
deck."

"Dead?" exclaimed Harry Linsay. "Did you say the man was dead?"

"Dead as a dried ling," replied Jack Radkin. "His face was badly mangled, and one of his arms was broken — indeed it was nearly pulled from the socket. Besides, he was so long in the water that even a grampus could not have stood it without coming up to blow."

"And what was the consequence of such an outrageous act? Why were you not all hanged for murder, as you deserved to be?" said Harry Linsay.

"Not so fast, young man. Our motives were good. Our object was to do justice, and dodge the law's delay. Besides, we did not mean to drown the fellow entirely; but only to give him a foretaste of what was coming. It was rather a hard case for him, and it might have gone hard with us, if the matter had ever been found out."

"No doubt of that, Jack; but how did you get out of the scrape?" asked Bob Randy.

"Why, when the business was over, and the body of the bloody-minded Lascar a couple of miles astern, the companion-way was opened, and Mr. Bolan was told that the steward had by some unknown means got loose from his lashings in the half-deck, had rushed up the ladder, forced aside the booby-hatch, shaken off the men who tried to secure him, and jumped overboard. This story was recorded in the log-book, and I suppose everybody believed it, of course, and asked no questions. But I know nothing about that, for I was impressed on board an English man-of-war, just as we made the Land's End, the lieutenant who boarded us having taken a fancy to the cut of my jib, declaring that I was just the chap to wait on the ward-room mess."

Further discussion was prevented by the loud call of the officer on deck, who shouted, "Eight bells! Call the watch!"

10

and the group of listeners to Jack Radkin's story was scattered as if a bomb-shell had fallen in the midst of it.

Mark Rowland's sufferings on the island of St. Paul, his prepossessing countenance, and his modest demeanor, and perhaps the fact that he was possessed of a goodly amount of riches, which, however acquired, in the eyes of short-sighted mortals, is apt to add to a man's respectability, gained him the favor of Captain Lamark and his officers. He messed in the cabin, and the kind treatment he received, and generous living, did wonders. In a week or ten days, he in a great measure recovered from the shock which his health and constitution had met with in consequence of exposures and hard fare on the island of St. Paul. He felt able as well as willing to work, and readily lent a hand to pull and haul, make and take in sail, or do any other similar duty.

Mark volunteered to join Mr. Hawkins's watch, for he felt deeply attached to that veteran sailor, who was the first person to take him by the hand, and give him words of comfort, after his long sojourn on the island. Mr. Hawkins, on his part, took a decided liking to Mark, and during the remainder of the voyage treated him with much kindness, seemed to regard him as a companion, answered all his questions, and in the long watches of the night related many incidents, and described scenes he had met with in the course of his eventful life, that gave Mark a deep insight into the mysteries of a sailor's occupation.

A few days after Mark Rowland had been on board the Rosamond, he described to Mr. Hawkins his plan of constructing a bathing-place in the island in order to avoid the sharks, and how it came to pass that some impertinent and ill-favored animals had invaded his domains, taken possession of his pond, and deprived him of his daily recreation. He minutely described their appearance, and added that he doubted not they were formidable and ferocious animals, half fish and half flesh; perhaps they were mermen or mermaids, and he congratulated himself on having escaped their clutches.

Mr. Hawkins indulged in a hearty laugh. "Why," said he, "they were only *seals*, an inoffensive animal, which would not harm an infant. With a small club you might have defended yourself against an army of them, if they could have mustered courage enough to attack you. In the South Sea Islands, I have seen hundreds of them lying on the rocks all dead or senseless, and ready to have their jackets stripped off, and their blubber put into the trying-pot, having been knocked on the head by a couple of sailors equipped for the work."

"But what business had they in my pond?" said Mark. "After I had fenced out the sharks, and put it in excellent order for a bathing-place, it was an act of unparalleled impudence on their part to appropriate it to themselves with so little ceremony, and try to frighten me away by defiant looks."

"They were probably wanderers in search of a resting-place," rejoined Mr. Hawkins, "having been driven from their homes in a much higher latitude, — for seals are seldom seen in the torrid zone, — or perhaps adventurers in quest of some new and unexplored region, with a view to found a colony. They may have been cruising round the island for some time before you were frightened by their ugly faces, and having discovered your cozy little pond, which, I dare say, was well stocked with fishes of various kinds, congratulated themselves on having realized a seal's idea of a Paradise on earth."

"If that's the case," said Mark, "it would have been a pity to disturb them, and they are heartily welcome to the pond. I shall never put in a claim for it hereafter. I hope they will long keep possession, and much good may it do them!"

"Spoken like a Christian," said Mr. Hawkins, "to which I say amen. Man has much to answer for in searching out their haunts in the most remote parts of the globe, and destroying millions of these harmless and interesting creatures, merely for their furs and oil. You made a great mistake in supposing they were mermen or mermaids, which are a very different order of beings. It was lucky you did not fall in with those strange creatures on that island."

"Why so?" inquired Mark.

"Because, if all tales be true, they are a treacherous and ungrateful race, hating mankind, and never so well pleased as when doing a sailor or a fisherman an ill turn."

"What kind of looking beasts are they?" said Mark.

"Their features bear a close resemblance to those of human beings," said Mr. Hawkins. "But the noses of the mermen have a curious twist to starboard. Their eyes are small, and they all squint, as if they were trying to look half a dozen ways at once, and their beards, of coarse texture and of a sea-green hue, reach to the waist. Their appearance, on the whole, is not prepossessing."

"So I should suppose," said Mark, with a smile.

"The mermen," continued Mr. Hawkins, "probably because their appearance is so very repulsive, seldom show themselves; but they may not be so bad as their looks indicate, after all. The worst rogues are often good-looking, while an honest man may wear an ugly phiz. Old Captain Lugner, whom I sailed with once in the ship Nonesuch, said that, on a passage to Batavia, he came in sight of the Martin Vas Rocks in the South Atlantic, when a merman swam off from the rocks, and after a great exertion, climbed up the ship's side, to the great consternation of the captain, mates, and all hands. On passing over the gangway, he made a polite bow, and inquired for the captain, who was pointed out to him by the boatswain, an old cross-grained man-of-war's man, who feared nothing in the shape of man or monster.

"The merman saluted the captain respectfully, and removing a bunch of seaweed from his starboard flipper, showed an ugly wound which was still bleeding. He said he had that morning had a fight with a ground shark, who had bitten off his apologies for fingers, and he begged Captain Lugner to favor him with a little of his surgical skill and assistance. The captain, who was a kind-hearted man, recovered from his fright, and went into the cabin, and brought up a roll of sticking-plaster, which he applied to the wounded part, and carefully bandaged it, telling his visitor the wound would soon heal. The merman, with a hideous grin intended to be particularly gracious, made a salaam, then turned a double somersault backwards over the quarter-rail into the water, and was off like a finback whale."

Mark Rowland stared hard at Mr. Hawkins, after listening to this strange story; but finding that worthy officer looking very serious, as if there could be no doubt of its truth, he resumed the conversation, by saying, "So much for the mer*men;* but of the mer*maids!* What of them?"

"Oh, they are said to be quite handsome, extremely so, with faces as round and smooth as an apple, with little turned-up noses, blue eyes which will look right through a man as a corkscrew goes through a cork, complexions thoroughly bleached in salt water, and clear and white as alabaster, and a great profusion of hair, hanging in tresses a yard and a half long, which they are often seen combing with the lower jaw-bone of a shark, while they are reclining among the rocks on some lonely shore, with their heads and shoulders only out of water."

10*

"They must be rare-looking creatures, indeed," said Mark. "But do they never leave the water entirely?"

"But seldom," replied Mr. Hawkins, "for only the upper half of their bodies is human; the rest is like that of a fish, and is terminated with a splendid fish-like tail. So you see the creatures cunningly contrive to keep the lower half of their bodies out of sight, lest it should make an unfavorable impression on those who might chance to see them."

"I think they are quite right in doing so," said Mark. "Can they talk intelligibly?"

"Certainly they can, and use honeyed words, too."

"What language do they speak?"

"What language? Why, all languages, of course. Address them in any tongue, and they will reply in the same. English, French, Dutch, Spanish, Italian, or even Choctaw, or Welsh, — 'tis all the same to them, and I doubt not that, in the language of the only poem I ever read, —

> "'—— they can speak Greek,
> As naturally as pigs do squeak;
> And Latin is no more difficile,
> Than for a blackbird 'tis to whistle.'

But their greatest charm is in their singing. They will lie for hours among the rocks, and sing a variety of enchanting songs, with voices that thrill through the heart of a man, and make him forget his best friends, his home, his wife and children, and draw him towards them by some strange but irresistible fascination, as the opossum is drawn towards the boa constrictor. But woe to him if he gets within reach of one of these treacherous beings! While he listens to the song with rapture, and advances towards her, his heart overflowing with gladness, she grasps him with her fin-like arms, exerting a strength that few have power to resist, and, to his great amazement and horror, plunges with him into the flood, and he is never seen again."

" But, Mr. Hawkins," inquired Mark, " suppose the man should be the stronger of the two?"

" He can keep her his prisoner, and feed her on fresh fish and salt water, until she grants him three wishes, which must not be altogether unreasonable, relating to success in his occupation or his domestic happiness."

Mark listened, with eyes wide open, to these marvellous statements; and after a pause of a few minutes, abruptly asked Mr. Hawkins, " Pray, sir, did *you* ever see a mermaid?"

" Well, no — yes — only once," replied Mr. Hawkins, in a manner exceedingly embarassed, an unusual case with him. " Upon the whole, Mark, I don't mind telling you all about it. The fact is, whatever my ' protection' may say, I was born and brought up in a small fishing village on the most rocky-bound coast of Nova Scotia. My father was a fisherman, as his father was before him, and I was educated to the same business; and at an early age became initiated into all the mysteries of the cod, mackerel, and herring fisheries. When quite young, being only eighteen years old, I fell in love with a bright-eyed little beauty, named Rosa Bell, who lived in our immediate neighborhood. It happened, unfortunately for my peace of mind, that Rosa proved to be a veritable coquette, and being much sought after by the young fishermen, and having several strings to her bow, hardly deigned to favor me with a smile, especially if other suitors were present. But I had heard of mermaids, and knew they had been seen at times on different parts of the coast. Indeed, I was assured by a very old fisherman that they sometimes visited a lonely, uninhabited island, just opposite my father's hut, and about a quarter of a mile from the main land. He said they had been seen sometimes in the edge of evening, sporting and making merry in the waters at the base of the overhanging cliffs, and if I kept a sharp lookout in that direction after sunset, I might be fortunate enough to see one, and if my strength and courage did not fail me, seize upon her and compel her to grant me three wishes.

"The idea was a bright one, and I resolved to profit by it without loss of time. With this object in view, I several times crossed over to the island stealthily in the afternoon, and as twilight approached, gazed inquiringly around, hoping to see a mermaid reposing on the rocks, or sporting in the water; and one memorable evening my expectations were realized.

"You can hardly conceive of the joy, of the trepidation, which seized me, when, just at dusk, I saw one of these beautiful creatures come out of the sea, and apparently much fatigued with the exercise of swimming, rest herself on a shelving rock. Her long hair, dripping with the salt water, hung down in long and thick tresses; and she immediately began to press out the water, and comb the tresses with her fingers.

"'Now is the time,' thought I to myself. 'If I don't embrace this opportunity, may I never get married.' I was young and vigorous, strong as a giant, and bold as a buffalo, and with such a prize as Rosa Bell at stake, did not for a moment hesitate to measure my strength with a mermaid, not more than half my size.' I crept down from my hiding-place, passed gently around a ledge of rocks, and came suddenly upon the unsuspecting water nymph. With one bound I was at her side. I caught her round the waist, and clutched her in my arms.

"She was dreadfully frightened, and gave a shrill and prolonged scream, which was heard a mile and a half off! She fought like a tiger-cat, and struggled hard to get away.

'Let me go! *Do* let me go!' she cried, in genuine fisherman's lingo. But it was of no use. Exerting all my
strength, I soon mastered her. 'Now,' said I, in a menacing
tone, 'grant me three wishes, here on the. spot, or you are
my prisoner for life. Here they are: first, I *wish* to marry
Rosa Bell, — secondly, I *wish* to own a neat cottage, handsomely furnished, — thirdly, I *wish* to have a hundred guin-
eas put in my pocket every New Year's Day. What say
you to that, now? Will you grant my wishes? Say *yes*, or
I'll —— ' "

" ' Oh, yes, yes,' said the mermaid, in a trembling voice.
'Let me go! *Do* let me go!' "

" ' That's enough,' said I; and as a mermaid was never
known to break her word, I instantly released her. The
moment my arms were unclasped, she made a dive beneath
the water, but to my surprise soon rose to the surface, her
head above the rippling waves, and began swimming like a
sea-horse towards the opposite shore.

" ' Never mind,' I said aloud, to myself, ' 'tis all right!
My three wishes are granted, and I am a made man for life.
Jemmy Hawkins and Rosa Bell forever! Success to the
mermaids! I skipped across the rocks, and reached my
skiff, which was lying quietly in a little cove, and crossed
over to the mainland, my heart as light as the down from
beneath. the wing of a diver, and my head actually bewildered with my good fortune. I hardly slept a wink that
night, but of waking dreams I had abundance, and they
were of the most gay and happy description. At an early
hour I sallied forth rejoicing, determined to take immediate
steps towards securing my good fortune.

" But my disappointment, shame, and mortification may
be imagined, when I learned that I had made a terrible mistake, and the whole village was in an uproar of merriment
about it. The little mermaid, who, after struggling and

fighting like a pirate, granted my three wishes, proved to be no mermaid after all, but a lively, frolicsome girl, real flesh and blood, named Polly Wogge, old skipper Wogge's youngest daughter. She was an adroit swimmer, and in a gay mood had left her companions sporting in the surf near the beach, and ventured across the smooth water to the island. Supposing herself alone, she intended resting for a while on the rock, after the fatiguing exercise, when I pounced upon, and nearly frightened her out of her wits.

"I could not stand the shafts of ridicule that were levelled against me. It was more than human nature could bear. Both Polly Wogge and Rosa Bell were unsparing in their taunts, gibes, and jests; and even the children laughed and pointed at me, as I passed the huts on my way to the shore. So I took a straight course for Halifax, worked my passage to Boston, shipped as a sailor on board a brig bound to the West Indies, and have never visited Nova Scotia since."

CHAPTER X

FOR several days after the ship Rosamond crossed the equator, the wind continued light and baffling, and sometimes for hours it was entirely calm. The ship gradually worked to the southward, however, and having reached the latitude of three degrees, the regular south-east trade winds began to blow, and the ship passed merrily on her way, close-hauled, with a pleasant six-knot breeze, a clear sky, and a smooth sea.

On the following morning, having reached the latitude of six degrees south, a ship was descried from aloft, about two points forward of the beam, and distant some six or seven miles. The ship was apparently on a wind, steering to the northward, and under short sail. The royals and top-gallant sails were furled, and the mainsail hauled up. Captain Lamark was called, and with spy-glass in hand he hastened on deck.

" That fellow don't seem to be in a hurry," said Mr. Hawkins, who had the morning watch. " I wonder where he is bound to in that direction, and why he don't make more sail."

" He may be from the River of Plate, bound to some port in Europe," said Captain Lamark ; " and as his masts have the true pilot-boat rake, and the captain is probably paid by the month, he jogs along quietly under easy sail, and will leave more wages due him at the end of the voyage than would be the case if he cracked on all sail in all weathers. Well, peace be with him; let him spin his own spunyarn. Hallo! what is the fellow about now? He's tacking ship as sure as I'm a porpoise, and his vessel goes round like a top!"

Captain Lamark's eyes did not deceive him. The stranger had by this time probably got a glimpse of the Rosamond, and seemed suddenly endued with new life. After having tacked ship, he kept off the wind a couple of points, set top-gallant sails and royals and studding-sails, steering in a direction that would enable him, if he proved the fastest sailer, to close with the Rosamond.

Captain Lamark watched him closely with his spy-glass, and was by no means satisfied with his appearance. The ship was a clipper, and gained upon us fast. As he drew nearer, Captain Lamark declared that the fellow looked like a rogue, for he carried guns, but could hardly be a man-of-war cruising in peaceable times in that part of the ocean.

"Perhaps," said Mr. Digges, "he is a Portuguese slaver, bound to some port in Brazil."

"Not very likely," remarked the captain. "If he is one of those man-stealers, he would not be steering away to the northward under a scarcity of canvas, but would be making a straight course for his destined port, under a press of sail. He is far more likely to be a slave-ship transformed into a pirate, — a transformation very natural, and easily effected. But in either case he must be an ugly customer, and we will try to give him a wide berth, and dodge him if possible."

Orders were now given to keep the ship off a couple of points, the yards were braced in and studding-sails set on the larboard side, and a hand-engine was put in operation for wetting the sails. There was a fine breeze, and the Rosamond began to slip through the water at the rate of nine or ten knots. The ship clearly did her best; and the great white bone she carried in her mouth, and the broad, bubbling, boiling wake she left behind, were marvellous to behold.

It was soon seen that our exertions were of no use. The stranger gained upon the Rosamond every minute. This being the case, Captain Lamark, who was distinguished for energy and courage, and was seldom at a loss for resources, turned his attention to the condition of his defences, not knowing how soon he might have a brush with an enemy.

The Rosamond had six carriage-guns on board, not of large calibre, being six-pounders, which had been well fitted with breechings and gun-tackles, after the ship reached the tropics, and plenty of ammunition, such as woollen cartridges, rope-yarn wads, and round shot, grape, and canister. The magazine was in the run, and contained several kegs of powder. There was also on board a good supply of muskets and boarding-pikes, so that a smart action could be maintained so long as there were men enough to manage the guns and wield the boarding-pikes. But it was manifest that the Rosamond had not a sufficient armament and crew to cope successfully with a piratical ship, heavily armed, with abundance of men to fight.

However, Captain Lamark ordered everything to be got in readiness for making a desperate resistance, provided the stranger should prove to be a rogue. The guns were loaded with round shot and canister. Every man knew his station. The captain declared he would sooner go to the bottom fighting boldly for life, than surrender like a craven, with the prospect of being shot through the head, or having his throat cut from ear to ear, in cold blood, as soon as the ship was boarded.. "Besides," said the captain, "remember that pirates are always cowards, and will fight hard only when it is necessary to save their necks from a halter. They never attack brave men who are provided with means of defence."

11

The strange sail continued to gain on the Rosamond, but hoisted no colors, and fired no gun. Captain Lamark now ordered the studding-sails and all the light sails to be taken in, and the courses hauled up, thus intimating to the stranger that, like a boxer who had stripped off all superfluous clothing, he was ready for a fight.

The three guns from the starboard side had been shifted over, and six ports having been opened, the guns were all ostentatiously run out, giving the peaceable old ship a decidedly warlike aspect. Pea-jackets and hats and caps were hung on handspikes, and paraded on different parts of the deck, looking mavellously like *men*, thus recruiting a strong force for the occasion with little trouble or expense; and half a dozen of the crew with muskets showed themselves on the quarter-deck, to increase the fierce and formidable appearance of the American East-Indiaman. Among these was Mark Rowland, who exhibited much intrepidity on the occasion, and seemed eager for the fight. " *Do* let me have a musket," said he to the captain. " I have more than once brought down a gray squirrel from the top of a lofty oak, and I know I can send a bullet through a pirate at more than double that distance." And his request was granted.

The suspicious vessel drew nearer. The men could be seen on the decks. It appeared to be about three hundred tons burden, but heavily sparred, and its masts had an unusual rake. It was evidently an armed ship, with men enough to work all the guns, and to spare. It was no man-of-war, for the discipline on board was very loose, as was seen by the set of the sails, the staying of the masts, and the general management of the ship. It was painted black, and its high poop and forecastle-deck indicated that if not a slaver, it had been engaged recently in the slave-trade.

The stranger having got nearly in the wake of the Rosamond, hauled close on a wind, steering a course almost parallel, and keeping about half a mile off. It was an anxious time. He showed no colors, thus demonstrating that he was no friend in want of information or assistance. There was something grim and repulsive in his very looks. He clearly meant mischief, and would be restrained only by the most bold and resolute conduct on the part of those brave men who, unable to escape by a clean pair of heels, desperately confronted him, like a stag at bay.

The stranger now slackened sail, and for some time kept along at the same distance, and on the weather-beam of the Indiaman, apparently undetermined what course to adopt. Meanwhile, the crew of the ship, trembling with suspense and excitement, but not with fear, stood boldly to their guns, ready at a word or a sign from the captain to pour in a broadside, and keep up the fight with the big guns, muskets, and boarding-pikes, as long as a man was left to load a gun or wield a weapon.

After running along in this manner some fifteen or twenty minutes, the piratical craft gradually edged away; and as the course of the Rosamond was not changed, the two vessels approached each other until almost within hail, being hardly a quarter of a mile apart. Mr. Digges, convinced that the fellow was a pirate, and believing that if he was not, he richly deserved to be chastised for his insolence, strongly urged Captain Lamark to hoist the Yankee flag and give him a broadside.

To this Captain Lamark objected, on the ground that there had yet been no hostile demonstration. "Keep cool, keep collected, Mr. Digges," said the captain, "and be ready for the word; and remember, that when we begin the work, we must put it through at all hazards, like true-blue American sailors!"

The pirate captain was easily distinguished, as he stood on the poop giving orders through his speaking-trumpet, and frequently using his spy-glass. He wore a striped shirt and white trousers, but neither jacket nor vest; he also wore a bandanna kerchief loosely around his neck, and a gray cap on his head. He took a close and deliberate survey, but did not seem to like the appearance of the ship. Preparations for a desperate resistance were too manifest to suit his purpose, which undoubtedly was booty without risk; for pirates in all ages dearly love to rob and murder, but not to fight. He fired a gun to windward as a note of defiance, and without showing any flag, tacked ship, and stood away to the northward under full sail.

When this manœuvre was executed, every man on board breathed easier. "We have had a narrow escape," said Captain Lamark. "It was lucky for us we could show *our teeth*, and were ready and willing to bite."

Only Mark Rowland expressed regret at the result. "Oh," said he, "I should *so* like to have had a shot at that pirate captain!"

That the ship, whose conduct was so mysterious, was a pirate, there was no doubt; for, on the arrival of Captain Lamark at the Cape of Good Hope, he learned that an English sloop-of-war had sailed from Cape Town only a few days before, to cruise near the equator for a pirate ship which infested the track of vessels bound to the East Indies and the Brazils. This ship, formerly a slaver from Havana, was commanded by a Spaniard notorious for his cruelty and ferocity and deadly hatred of Britons and Americans, on account of their interference with the slave-trade. For these fiendish traits of character, he received, and was generally known by, the significant appellation of "Der Teufel." And before the Rosamond reached the Cape of Good Hope, as will be seen hereafter, her crew met with fearful evidence that some inhuman monsters were cruising in that part of the South Atlantic, and committing startling, bloody, and fiend-like deeds.

That night, in the first watch, the sailors on duty were grouped together on the forecastle, talking over the incidents of the day, or indulging in speculations respecting the character of the stranger who had given them so much trouble, and caused them so much perplexity and fear.

" We may thank the kind Providence that watches over sailors," said Jack Radkin, " that we escaped from the · clutches of that fellow. If a gun had been fired on either side, it would have brought on a battle, and we should have come off second best, and been food for sharks long before this. Those Guineamen are desperate men. I know them of old. When they turn pirates, they fight like demons, and massacre, in hot or cold blood, every being — man, woman, or child — who falls into their hands."

" You know them of old?" inquired Abram Hartshorn. " Were you ever in a slaver, Jack?"

" Not exactly," replied the old tar; " but I've been in a British man-of-war on a cruise after slavers, and have witnessed scenes on the coast of Guinea that gave me an insight into their character, — scenes almost too horrible to describe."

" What were they, Jack? Tell us all about them," clamorously exclaimed his watchmates, who dearly loved a yarn, and rejoiced at the prospect of having one spun by Jack Radkin.

" I have already told you," said the veteran sailor, " that when I was a boy, hardly knee-high to a marline-spike, I was impressed, for my sins, on board an English frigate in the chops of the English Channel. A few weeks afterwards, we entered Plymouth, and I was drafted on board the gun-brig Porcupine, commanded by Lieutenant James Throgmorton, and mounting twelve guns, a remarkably fast vessel, bound

11*

on a cruise to the coast of Africa, to look after the man-
stealing craft in that quarter, with instructions to capture
or destroy all we might fall in with.

"After touching at Sierra Leone, we cruised for a while
in the Bight of Benin, afterwards in the Gulf of Biafra;
and although we did not succeed in capturing any of the
slavers sneaking out of the creeks and lagoons, with full
cargoes of negroes, we had the satisfaction of knowing that
we prevented several suspicious-looking armed clippers from
stealing in. Two clipper-brigs, which, from appearances,
were undoubted Guineamen, being completely fitted up and
in readiness to receive a large cargo of darkies, we captured, after a running fight, and sent to Sierra Leone for
condemnation.

"We afterwards proceeded down the coast some five hundred miles, with a view to look into Loango and Kabinda,
or blockade the mouth of the Congo river. We arrived off
Kabinda early one morning, and saw a ship in the offing,
which had evidently left the harbor a few hours before, with
all sail set, steering to the westward, with a light breeze
from the north-east.

"'Hallo,' said the captain, after eyeing the ship for a
while through his spy-glass, 'yonder is one of the rogues
we are after; a ship full of negroes, real Congoes, stowed in
bulk! Now we have another chance to try what stuff the
Porcupine is made of. Clap on every stitch of canvas that
will draw,' said he to the lieutenant. .'Before the blessed
sun sinks into his briny bed that ship must be a prize to the
Porcupine, and the skipper, officers, and crew, clapped in
double irons, as sure as my name is Throgmorton!'

"His orders were promptly obeyed. We soon reached
the wake of the slave-ship, and with an unsteady breeze,
directly aft, and under a cloud of sail, continued the chase.

"The slave-ship was a clipper, as is the case with all

vessels engaged in that detestable traffic, but was better calculated to work to windward than run before the wind.
While, on the contrary, the Porcupine, a fast vessel, built on
a different model, with a good breeze in her wake, and studding-sails, both sides, alow and aloft, and a smooth sea,
would slip along through the water as fast as any ship that
ever was built. The slaver, I've no doubt, would have
given all his old junk and a good part of his cargo besides,
to have got the weather-gage. But it could not be. It was
a fair race, — *dead before the wind*, — and all he had to do
was to crowd on all his canvas, steer small, and trust to
luck and his six-pounders.

"The slaver had some six or eight miles the start, — a
great advantage, — and the wind being light, for some time
the result was uncertain. Captain Throgmorton was greatly
excited. The sails were stretched to the utmost. Impossible plans were resorted to in order to spread more canvas,
and set studding-sails outside of studding-sails, and if hal-
looing, swearing, and stamping could have helped us, we
should have been alongside the ship in no time.

"But the breeze increased, and when in the course of half
an hour it became evident that we were slowly but surely
gaining on the chase, the captain's exultation knew no
bounds. 'We shall catch the rascal!' said he to his first
lieutenant. 'He cannot escape us now. See the guns all
loaded and double-shotted, for these desperadoes, when they
cannot run away, will stand at bay and fight like pirates.'

"But the wind soon afterwards died away, and for an hour
or two we drew no nearer. Then the breeze freshened again,
and then it lulled, and we had cats-paws and fresh breezes
by turns, until about three o'clock in the afternoon, when we
had approached the ship so closely that the captain ordered
a shot to be sent from a twelve-pounder mounted on the bow.
The ball passed over the ship, doing no harm, and the slaver

instantly acknowledged the compliment and returned it, by
sending towards us the contents of his stern-chasers, which,
however, fell short.

"The wind, although light, was now more steady, and
Captain Throgmorton was excessively anxious to close with
and capture the chase before night, lest the rascal should
give us the slip in the dark. On the other hand, the slaver
left no means untried to baffle our efforts. The two guns of
small calibre that the ship fired from time to time from the
stern ports, did little or no execution, for they were badly
served, while it was evident that our twelve-pounder, which
struck the ship several times, did considerable damage,
making the splinters fly in every direction, and must have
cut off all hopes of escape. The prospect was now good
that Captain Throgmorton's prediction would be realized,
and the slave-ship would become a prize to his Majesty's
brig Porcupine, and all the crew in irons before night. But
we did not know the true character of the slavers, and could
not even dream of the desperate means they would resort to
in order to avoid being captured.

"Captain Throgmorton, who was standing on the forecastle watching every movement of the slave-ship through his
spy-glass, suddenly gave orders in a very excited tone, and
apparently without a shadow of reason, 'Stand by, lads! in
studding-sails! haul up the courses! brace up the head-yards,
and be handy about it! hard a-starboard your helm, Jack!'
and in two minutes the brig was lying-to, motionless on the
water, with the maintop-sail aback.

"Orders were now given to man and lower away one of
the boats; and the sight of several dark-looking objects in
the water, but a few fathoms to leeward, looking like cocoa-
nuts or calibashes bobbing up and down, gave us a glimpse
of the cause of this strange proceeding. It seems that the
black-hearted villain, finding we were fast overhauling him,

had thrown overboard some half a dozen negroes, knowing that they could swim, and that we, through a feeling of humanity, would heave-to, get out our boats, and pick them up, while in the mean time the ship would be sailing onward, and rapidly increasing the distance between us.

" The trick was successful. The poor negroes were saved, and brought on board the Porcupine, and then in a jiffey we were again under all sail in chase. On again drawing near the ship, the trick was repeated, with the same result. It now looked as if the slaver might manage in this way to avoid capture until dark, and perhaps in the end make his escape.

" But Captain Throgmorton was not to be thus cheated out of his prize. At the third time of heaving-to, he ordered the launch to be hoisted out, and manned by an officer and eight seamen, with orders to pick up all the negroes he could find, and follow in the wake of the brig. He declared that he would not heave-to again, if the whole cargo of blacks was thrown overboard; that it was better even to sacrifice a few lives, than allow such an unmitigated villain as the commander of that vessel must be, to escape the punishment he deserved.

" So we sailed straight on for the ship, and as the breeze increased, drew towards it, hand over hand. Meanwhile the slaver continued to pitch negroes overboard, and the launch astern was busily employed in picking them up. We kept peppering the slaver with our bow-guns, and, giving an occasional yaw, would let fly a whole broadside, which cut up her rigging, must have made bloody work with the crew, and finally tumbled the maintop-mast over the side, and put an end to the chase. The ship, whose guns had been silenced for the last half hour, now rounded to, and hoisted a Portuguese flag, and immediately hauled it down, in token of surrender.

" In a few minutes both vessels were lying-to, almost

within hail of each other, and a boat with an officer and a large party of armed men was dispatched from the Porcupine to take possession of the slave-ship. The boat reached the side of the ship, and the men were mounting the gangway ladder, when Captain Throgmorton and all the Porcupine's crew were gazing eagerly at the slaver, anxious to see what kind of a reception our friends would meet with.

"We were not long kept in suspense. Just as the officer was stepping over the gangway, with the boat's-crew at his heels, a dense volume of smoke rose suddenly from the quarter-deck, followed by a cloud of masts, sails, timbers, and human beings, some of which were shot high into the air, and others were spread out on every side, and then fell in a fearful shower, disturbing the ocean for half a mile around.

"The captain of the slave-ship, finding there were no hopes of escape, and being a desperate ruffian, crazy with disappointment and rage, had fired the powder in the magazine, and blown the ship sky-high.

"The explosion was an awful one. It made old ocean tremble for miles around, and actually shook the timbers of the Porcupine. The brig was still shaking when the sky above us seemed to open, deluging our decks with pieces of wreck, showers of gore, and human trunks and limbs.

"The slaver had a ship's company consisting of thirty-five men, all told, belonging to half a dozen nations, and was commanded by a Portuguese named Pedro Martinez, and bound for San Salvador in the Bay of All Saints. There was a full cargo on board, consisting of six hundred negroes, who all perished by this dreadful explosion, excepting about a half dozen, who were drawn out from among the fragments of the wreck, some of them badly wounded, and those who were thrown overboard during the chase, and picked up by our boats. Only one of the ship's company was saved; and he was found clinging to a spar, with his thigh broken. Of the officer and boat's crew who boarded the slaver, no trace was ever discovered.

" So much for these slave-ships, shipmates. And when such fellows turn pirates, and hoist the black flag, you may imagine what demons they become, and how terrible would be our fate if we should fall into such hands. May the time never come when we shall be compelled to call upon such monsters for mercy ! "

" I say amen to that," exclaimed Bob Randy.

" So say we all," added his watch-mates.

CHAPTER XI.

On the evening after the exciting chase and preparations made for fighting for life, described in the foregoing chapter, the captain and mates were talking over the affair on the quarter-deck, while the ship was slipping along through the water at the rate of six or seven knots.

"Captain Lamark, that was a bright idea of yours," said Mr. Digges, the chief mate, "that of dressing up the handspikes with pea-jackets and caps, and thus doubling the number of our crew."

"Yes," said Mr. Hawkins; "it must have been that which frightened the pirate. He was afraid to board us in the face of such a number of desperate men, well armed and fighting for their lives. Not wishing to risk the loss of half his crew, he wisely made off, and left us alone in our glory."

"The scheme was a good one," said the captain. "I had seen it tried before. This is not the first time I have fallen in with a pirate."

"Indeed!" exclaimed Mr. Digges.

"By no means," replied Captain Lamark, "and he was driven off by bluff and bravado, by handspikes and women transformed into sailors, and a living 'Long Tom.'"

"A *living* Long Tom? Surely, sir," exclaimed Mr. Digges, "you mean a wooden one."

"No such a thing," said the captain. "I will tell you

132

how the affair took place. When I was a youngster, I shipped as an ordinary seaman on board the schooner Dandelion, bound from Charleston to Matanzas with a cargo of rice. The schooner was a good-looking vessel, with a flush deck, and sat deeply in the water, and being painted black made quite an imposing appearance. But although a good sailing vessel, she had no pretensions to being a clipper.

" The Dandelion was commanded by a little man with a long name, Cornelius Montgomery Duncannon. He was small in size, but full of energy and spirit. He was alive all over, in his muscles and bones, as well as in his brains and heart. Besides the captain, there belonged to the schooner the mate, Mr. Ramsey, four seamen, a boy, and a cook. There were also eight passengers on board, — three gentlemen and five ladies, — the whole number of persons on board being sixteen.

" Although many piracies had been committed on the coast of Cuba, the Dandelion was furnished with no means of defence; but was destitute of large guns, boarding-pikes, and cutlasses. Her sole stock of arms and ammunition consisted of three rusty muskets, and a flask of damaged powder.

" Off the Double-Headed Shot Keys, however, the folly and guilt of going to sea without arms became manifest. At sunrise one morning, a small schooner, long and low, with rakish masts, and a snakish appearance, with two or more guns run out of her port-holes, and her decks crowded with men, was descried leaving the Salt-Cay Bank, and making a straight course for the Dandelion. It was as clear as a moonlight night in Baffin's Cay, that mischief was afoot.

" The news was soon spread through the vessel that a pirate was in chase of the Dandelion, under full sail, and rapidly coming up. Great was the commotion on board. There was no occasion to call all hands; every man was on deck gazing at the schooner, almost before Captain Duncannon

had made her out through the spy-glass. The passengers,
also, impelled by fear and curiosity, tumbled upon deck,
scantily clad, and huddled around the captain, eagerly asking if that vessel was really a pirate.

"Captain Duncannon told them candidly that there was
cause for alarm; that the vessel undoubtedly *was* a pirate,
with intentions to board the Dandelion and commit outrages
on property and life; that he hardly knew how he could prevent it, as he could neither fight nor run; that he would *try*,
however, to disappoint the demons, and might perhaps hit
upon some pretext or plan to frighten the rascals, and save
the schooner, with the lives and property entrusted to his
care.

"'I was a fool and a blockhead,' said Captain Duncannon,
striking his forehead with his fist, ' to leave Charleston without something in the shape of a gun. If we had only a son
of a gun on board, or even a *Quaker*, it would be better
than nothing. We might manage to make the fellow think
it was Long Tom, when such is their dread of that gentleman, that he would wear round on his heel, get on the other
tack, and clear out like the Flying Dutchman in a gale of
wind. Oh, if we only had a Long Tom, although it were a
wooden one!'

"'Long Tom?' echoed Mr. Ramsay, the mate; ' a wood-
en one? Why would not a *living* one answer? Long Livingston would make a better one than was ever hewed out of a
block of wood!'

"'Long Livingston!' shouted the skipper, in a voice of
exultation, while the clouds vanished from his brow like a
fog before a sunbeam off Cape Sable. 'Long Livingston!
The very thing. Mr. Ramsay, you are a trump, and I was
a ninny not to have thought of it myself. Long Livingston
was fashioned by nature for a Long Tom. I have it now,
and if I do not astonish those fellows I am mistaken, that's all.'

" Long Livingston was the name given to one of the sailors, a tall, simple, ungainly looking Yankee, from ' down east.' IIis real name was Jacob Livingston; but on account of his height, being about six feet and a half, and remarkably slim, he was known on board by no other name than Long Livingston. IIe was a good-natured, harmless fellow, a standing target for a joke, and took in good part the shafts of wit that were from time to time levelled at him from every man on board.

" Captain Duncannon, with that alacrity in ferreting out and adopting resources which is peculiar to men of genius, at once seized upon the hint which his mate had given, and at the same time seized upon Livingston himself, with the laudable determination to transform that tall and interesting specimen of salt-water humanity into a ' Long Tom.' Livingston was astonished at being so suddenly changed from a quiet, peaceful, inoffensive sailor, into a formidable weapon of war, whose mission it was to pour forth vengeance, fury, fire, and brimstone, on the enemy. He made no objection, however. If Captain Duncannon thought he should make a good Long Tom, he had nothing to say against it.

" It happened, fortunately for those on board the Dandelion, that the wind was far to the northward, and the schooner was now running along with a five or six knot breeze, with the main boom guyed out on the larboard quarter. The pirate vessel being under the lee, those on board were unable to see any of the doings between the fore and main-mast of the schooner. Under Captain Duncannon's directions a platform was laid on the long boat in a marvellous short time. On the centre of this platform a log of wood, about two and a half feet long, sawed square off at each end, was placed upright and securely fixed. On the upper end a plank about seven feet long was placed horizontally. This plank was fastened to the top of the log, which acted as a pivot by a bolt, so that the position of the plank, that is, the direction in which it pointed, could be changed at will. To this plank long Livingston was lashed, having on his head a Scotch cap, which bore a strong resemblance to the muzzle of a big gun. A piece of rattlin stuff was tied to his heels, by hauling on which, this formidable piece of artillery, so promptly manufactured, and christened ' Long Tom,' could be slewed round like a teetotum.

" This work was soon accomplished, for when a man's life is at stake, it is astonishing how lively he works ; all his faculties seem sharpened, and he becomes endowed with ten-fold more ingenuity, skill, intellect, and muscle, than he ever before dreamed of possessing.

" While the process of manufacturing a live twenty-four-pounder was going on, another change, almost as great, was taking place in another quarter. Agreeably to a hint from Captain Duncannon, caps, tarpaulin hats, and checked shirts, were in demand, and almost before a leadsman could sing out, ' By the deep nine,' the eight passengers, and as many handspikes, were transformed into sixteen trig-looking sailors, all of them, *apparently*, ready and able to fight des-perately for their lives. The ladies were frightened, it must be confessed, and looked shockingly pale, and two of them could hardly stand without assistance. Nevertheless, they and the masquerading handspikes were stationed at points where they could *show* to the most advantage, and helped to swell the numbers of the crew to a very respectable extent.

" The transformation effected, and Long Tom finished, Captain Duncannon ordered a barrel, with the head knocked out, to be placed in the waist, and stationed three men near it with the loaded muskets, and orders to put the muzzles within the barrels, and, when the word was given, *fire!* He also stationed a couple of men in the top-mast cross-trees, each with a bucket of dry ashes, with instructions to empty the buckets and scatter the ashes in every direction, the moment the order to fire was given.

"By this time the suspicious-looking vessel, that glided through the water like a dolphin after a ballyhoo, had approached within a mile of the Dandelion, and, with his spyglass, Captain Duncannon could see all the doings on deck, which left no doubt on his mind that the vessel was a pirate, well armed, and with her decks full of men.

"He saw that no time was to be lost, and, after a word of encouragement to the green hands he had just shipped, he gave orders to jibe ship. The main peak was dropped, the helm put a-starboard, and the top-sail yard squared; the schooner fell off rapidly, soon took the breeze on the other quarter, and in a minute and a half was standing to the eastward, nearly close-hauled, and the pirate about four points on the weather-bow. 'Long Tom' was plainly in sight from the pirate's decks; also the somewhat numerous crew, stationed in groups at different points, and apparently ready, not only to repel boarders, but, when the time came, to board in their turn.

"At this critical moment Captain Duncannon waved his hand ostentatiously, as if to command attention, and shouted, in a loud voice, 'FIRE!' The muskets were discharged into the empty barrels, making a loud reverberating noise, and at the same moment the ashes were scattered in mid-air by the sailors in the cross-trees; and the imitation of a vast volume of smoke, belching forth from the muzzle of Long Tom, was perfect.

"The stars and stripes were now proudly waving from the peak, and Long Tom was trailed and managed, as if with the intention of giving the pirate a shot in earnest. But this was hardly necessary. The smoke had not cleared away, before the pirate, who, believing he 'had caught a Tartar,' and was terribly frightened at such a display of war-

12*

like force and courage, tacked ship, clapped on all sail, and made tracks for the Salt-Key Bank as fast as possible, doubtless expecting every minute to be hailed by a twenty-four-pound shot from the muzzle of Long Tom.

"The shot was not sent. The Dandelion continued the pursuit a short time, and then resumed her course. Long Livingston was released from his confinement to the plank, and highly and deservedly complimented for the admirable and successful manner in which he had enacted the important part allotted him in the engagement with the pirates; the handspikes were stripped of their hats and jackets; the ladies doffed their sailor's garbs, and resumed their more comely feminine attire, and one of them, a lively, laughing, frolicsome girl of eighteen summers, who had been terribly frightened during the chase, was so impressed with the magnitude of her obligations to Long Livingston, that she reached up her white arms, and, clasping him around the neck, gave him a hearty kiss. Livingston was astonished, and grinned with delight at such a rich and unexpected mark of approbation, and declared himself fully repaid for all the inconvenience he had suffered from being so long lashed to a plank. The next day we arrived safely in Matanzas."

"There is nothing like wisdom gained from experience," was the sententious remark of Mr. Digges.

"Yes," remarked Mr. Hawkins; "experience and sound, practical, old-fashioned, common sense will do wonders sometimes."

On the day after the adventure with the pirate, in the middle of the afternoon, one of the men at work on the forecastle shouted aloud, "Sail ho! On the lee bow!"

The sail was soon made out to be a brig, not more than five or six miles off, and her appearance was quite remarkable and alarming. She seemed to be steering no particular course, but was not lying-to. Her sails were flying loose in every direction; her maintop-mast was broken short off in the middle; her studding-booms were still rigged out forward, with the studding sails hanging in mid-air. The brig was abandoned to the winds and the waves; there was clearly no controlling power on board.

Captain Lamark took a keen survey of the brig through his glass, and then mused for a few minutes in silence, when his eye kindled, and an unwonted expression of ferocity rested on his features.

"What do you make her out to be, sir?" inquired Mr. Digges. "She seems to be acting rather queerly."

"There's more there than meets the eye," said Mr. Hawkins.

"There is, indeed!" remarked Captain Lamark, in a deep and solemn tone. "*That brig has been boarded by pirates!*" and turning round, he called aloud to the helmsman, "Keep her off, Jack, two or three points. So! That will do. Steer directly for that vessel ahead. Mr. Digges, we'll take a pull of the weather-braces."

"But, Captain Lamark," said Mr. Digges, in a remonstrating tone, "don't you think there may be danger in —— "

"Brace in the yards, Mr. Digges!" responded the captain, in a voice of thunder. "Danger! Who cares for danger in a time like this? I tell you that the pirate we fell in with yesterday has been busy at his bloody work; but we may not be too late to save the lives of some of his unfortunate victims."

The Rosamond with a free wind now went rapidly through the water, and in little more than half an hour had approached almost within hail of the brig; but not a human being was seen on her decks; yet ever and anon a loud and prolonged moan, half scream and half howl, a most unearthly and uncanny sound, came across the water from the direction of the brig, and sent a chill through every heart.

"What is the meaning of that wild and hideous cry?" exclaimed the captain.

"It is hard to say, sir," replied Mr. Hawkins; "but with your leave I'll go and see."

Orders were now given to heave the ship to; and in a few minutes the second mate, with four stout sailors, in the ship's yawl, was rapidly going towards the brig. As they drew near, shot-holes in the counter, and the shattered condition of the bulwarks, as well as the broken top-mast and fluttering sails, all told a fearful tale which could not be misunderstood of a running fight and a desperate but bootless resistance.

The loud unnatural sound, an unequivocal signal of distress, which had been heard from time to time before the boat left the brig, was now kept up without ceasing, and became frightfully discordant. The men looked hard at Mr. Hawkins, and slackened their labors as if wishing and expecting him to forego his intention to board the brig.

But the mate seemed all the more eager to be alongside. "Give way, my lads, and never heed that noise," said he, encouragingly. "Music like that, although it grates harshly on the ear, can break no bones! Ah! I understand it all now! There is one honest fellow alive on board that brig, at all events; and he is telling us in his way a woful story."

The men turned their heads towards the brig, and their fears vanished, when they saw standing with his fore-paws on the taffrail and stretching his head over the water towards the boat, a large black Newfoundland dog, whose incessant cries and howls had been the cause of their alarm.

"There has been terrible work here!" exclaimed Mr. Hawkins, as the boat ranged alongside the brig.

At that moment the dog leaped over the bulwarks, and

came tumbling down into the boat, and sprang upon the men, licking their faces, wagging his tail and yelping with delight.

"Harry Linsay," said the mate, "stay in the boat and take care of her. The rest of you, follow me!" and he climbed up the side of the brig and over the bulwarks, closely followed by the men.

And a dreadful sight they beheld. A bloody conflict had taken place. The scuppers were even then streaming with gore. The bodies of four men lay about the decks disfigured with ghastly gun-shot or sabre wounds. Two men, probably officers of the brig, were found each lashed to a plank, which had been set in an upright position and secured to the fife-rail, and made to serve as living targets for the pirates. The heads and bodies were perforated with dozens of pistol bullets.

The long-boat had been removed, and the hatchways taken off. The cargo had been broken into. The cabin doors were open, and Mr. Hawkins, after asking in a loud voice if there was any living person on board, and receiving no reply, passed down the cabin stairs into the cabin. On the cabin floor, near the doorway, lay the body of a man, whose dress and appearance indicated that he was the captain of the brig. His arms were pinioned, and his throat was cut from ear to ear.

Scattered over the floor were a woman's garments, and on the farther part of the cabin floor, at the entrance of a state-room, was the dead body of a woman, young and beautiful, almost entirely destitute of clothing, with a deep wound in her bosom, her long hair dishevelled and dabbled in blood, and an expression of horror on her features, which once seen could never be forgotten.

The cabin had been ransacked by the pirates; trunks and chests broken open, and doubtless everything of value carried away. Mr. Hawkins found the log-book on the transom, from which it appeared that the brig was the Angelica, Captain Melton, belonging to Bristol, in England, and bound from Montevideo to London. It appeared, according to the latest date in the log-book, that hardly eight-and-forty hours had elapsed since the pirates, after a desperate engagement, for the brig carried two carriage-guns, and probably was well furnished with muskets, gained possession of the vessel, killed or threw overboard all her crew, and committed other outrages too atrocious to record.

The brig appeared to be in a sinking condition, doubtless owing to a shot between wind and water, and Mr. Hawkins, finding that nothing could be done to keep her afloat, and that all the unfortunate men who composed the crew had been suddenly sent by the bloody-minded wretches to render their accounts at the judgment-seat of God, took the log-book under his arm, ordered the men, who had been standing on deck, paralyzed with horror, into the boat, and accompanied by the faithful, terrified, half-starved Newfoundland dog, returned to the ship.

Captain Lamark listened in silence to Mr. Hawkins, while he narrated the shocking scenes he had witnessed on board the brig. He was greatly moved, and shuddered as he thought how narrowly he himself and the gallant men who composed his crew, and looked to him for advice and protection, had escaped a similar fate. " Mr. Hawkins," said he, suddenly, " the brig will doubtless soon be full of water; but it does not follow that the hulk will immediately sink. If there is a buoyant cargo in the hold, it may be floating about for months, to the great danger of vessels navigating these seas. Besides, such a terrible evidence of human wickedness, ought to be removed from the sight of day as soon as possible. Therefore, man the boat once more and go back to that ill-fated vessel; take a lantern with you, and set her on fire."

The captain's orders were promptly obeyed; and when the boat left the brig the second time, smoke was seen issuing from various parts of the vessel, and soon a livid stream of light crept aloft, and the whole vessel was in flames.

The Rosamond stood on her course towards the Cape of Good Hope; but long after the sun had sank beneath the horizon, the light of the burning vessel could be seen illuminating the atmosphere and the surface of the water for miles around. But through the night a cloud rested on the minds of the crew of the ship; and silent prayers went up to heaven for the souls of those who had been so ruthlessly murdered, and grateful thanksgivings for their own preservation from a terrible death at the hands of the pirates.

CHAPTER XII.

THE Rosamond continued her course to the southward, close-hauled on the wind, which for several days blew steadily from the south-east. But soon after leaving the tropics the trade-wind failed, and variable winds exerted their power. Mr. Hawkins, in the night watches, pointed out and explained to Mark Rowland the marked changes in the aspect of the heavenly bodies; the splendid constellation of the Southern Cross, and those wild and weird-looking phenomena known as the Magellan clouds. The cape pigeons also began to come round the ship, and with a hook baited with a piece of pork, and attached to a line thrown over the stern, several of the foolish birds were caught, and served up in a sea-pie, which was not altogether to the liking of Mark, for it had a most ancient and fish-like flavor. As they drew towards the cape, the large, stately-looking albatrosses, some with wings extending twelve or fifteen feet across from tip to tip, were numerous, flying or floating in the wake of the ship, hoping, and not always in vain, to pick up savory morsels that had been thrown overboard.

One afternoon, as the ship was quietly proceeding on her way with a fair wind and a smooth sea, the man at the wheel created quite a sensation by crying out, "A shark!" and on looking in the direction in which he pointed, the dorsal fin and part of the tail of a large fish were seen above the water.

"Where's the shark-hook?" exclaimed Mr. Hawkins, with his accustomed energy; "cook, bring along a piece of pork from the harness-cask."

The captain, coming on deck at that moment, put a damper on the ardor of the second mate. "'Tis of no use, Mr. Hawkins," said he, after taking a look at the strange fish. "That is no shark, but a sword-fish; and they seldom take the hook."

Mr. Hawkins, however, baited the hook and threw it overboard, and towed it astern for a while, but it had no attractions for the stranger, who swam along near the surface, in a course parallel to that of the ship, and eight or ten fathoms off, for a few minutes, and then disappeared, to the great disappointment and disgust of the mate, who took intense delight in hooking or spearing the prowling inhabitants of the deep.

About two hours afterwards, just at the beginning of twilight, the ship experienced a sudden shock, as if the bottom had come in contact with some hard substance. Every man felt the jar, and sprang to his feet; while those who were below hastened on deck. Captain Lamark rushed up from the cabin, and, addressing the two officers, who were standing on the quarter-deck, said, "Mr. Digges, Mr. Hawkins, what does this mean? Has the ship struck a rock, or a shoal, or a sunken wreck? Get up the deep sea-lead, and we will take a sound."

In a few minutes, while Mr. Hawkins was getting in readiness the sounding apparatus, the captain remarked in a more quiet tone, "It is hardly worth while to sound, for there is no sign of breakers, and, if there is any truth in the charts, there is neither rock nor shoal within hundreds of miles."

The lead, however, was thrown overboard, but no bottom was found with one hundred and twenty fathoms of line.

13

All at once Captain Lamark struck his forehead violently with his fist. "I have it now!" he cried. "It was that confounded sword-fish! He has mistaken the peaceable Rosamond for a pugnacious sperm whale, and, with his horn, has struck the bottom of the ship with what he intended should be a mortal blow. But I trust he has got the worst of it."

That evening Mark Rowland, who had never before heard of a sword-fish, and whose curiosity was greatly excited, made some inquiries of Captain Lamark relative to the appearance and habits of this bold animal, which, without any provocation, would venture to attack a ship or a whale.

"The sword-fish," said Captain Lamark, "is occasionally met with in every sea; but more frequently on soundings than in deep water. One of its favorite haunts is the shoals off the island of Nantucket. It is also often seen on St. George's Bank. It is quite a large fish, measuring from nine to fifteen feet in length, and sometimes weighing six hundred pounds. From its upper jaw a horn, or sword, as it is called, projects two or three feet, according to the size of the fish, and gives a name to the animal. This horn is pointed, and is composed of a hard, fibrous substance, bearing but little resemblance to ivory. It does not seem to be of any use to its owner in procuring food, as this fish feeds principally on mackerel, herring, flying-fish, and other small varieties of the inhabitants of the deep. Nor can this sword be regarded as a necessary weapon of defence, for such is the size, strength, and activity of the sword-fish, that it need fear no attack from any fish that swims. And unless we look upon it as an ornament, we must regard it as a strictly offensive weapon, as it probably is.

"It is generally believed that the sword-fish is the mortal enemy of the whale, and attacks him with great fury, without provocation, whenever they meet, plunging his sword into the throat in such a manner that the water is soon dyed red with the blood of his victim, whose convulsive exertions to escape from his vindictive enemy are vain; and, conquered by a comparatively weak and humble opponent, he dies ignobly.

"This is an unamiable trait in the character of the sword-fish, and there are those who contend that injustice is done him in this respect. It is nevertheless confirmed by the fact that the sword-fish will sometimes strike the bottom of a ship with great violence, which can only be accounted for on the supposition that the fish mistakes the ship for some huge monster which he is in the habit of regarding as a mortal foe. The sword-fish has been known to attack a ship with such desperate violence as to thrust his horn through the planks, even into the hold of the vessel; but as the fish cannot disengage it, the horn of course is broken off, doubtless greatly to the rage and mortification of the fish, and remains in the plank into which he had so unthinkingly thrust it, and thus plugs up the hole it had made.

"The fishermen living on the islands lying to the southward of Cape Cod, take a considerable number of sword-fish every season. As this fish swims near the surface, and his back-fin sticks sometimes a foot out of water, he is easily discovered. Not being a shy fish, he is generally captured by striking him with a harpoon, to which a strong line is attached, a feat which requires considerable skill; and sometimes he is taken with a strong line and halibut-hook, using a mackerel for bait. The flesh of the sword-fish is considered good eating, and a couple of hundred barrels are taken every year by the fishermen of Nantucket and Martha's Vineyard, cut into slices, pickled, or salted and sold.

"I have no doubt," said Captain Lamark, in concluding his remarks about the sword-fish, "that when we discharge our cargo in Table Bay, we shall find a sword as long as my arm sticking in the ship's bottom!"

And the captain was not far out of the way. When the cargo was discharged it was found difficult to disengage from its resting-place on the ceiling, near the kelson, a large box containing furniture. When it was at last wrenched away, it was found that the horn of the sword-fish had passed through the copper sheathing of the ship and a three-inch oak plank, between a couple of timbers, and through another plank, two and a half inches in thickness, and had penetrated the box, pinning a bureau to the position assigned it by the stevedores.

As the Rosamond approached the Cape of Good Hope, the weather, which had been tempestuous, became moderate, with light breezes from the eastward. Such weather was unusual in that quarter, and did not correspond with the name given to it by that bold navigator, Bartholomew Diaz, who discovered it in the fifteenth century, and in consequence of the furious tempests which continually raged in that vicinity, called it *Cabo Tormentoso*, the Cape of Storms.

One day, when about a couple of days' sail from Cape Town, and just as Captain Lamark had proclaimed that it was twelve o'clock, and Mr. Hawkins had ordered the cook to give the men their dinner, Jack Radkin, who was at the wheel, said to the captain, in a tone tremulous through excitement, "Captain Lamark, there is something in the water, there ahead. I believe it is a boat!"

The captain called to the steward for his spy-glass, and ran forward to the forecastle to obtain a better view. The object proved to be a boat floating on the water, not half a mile off, and directly ahead. As no persons were seen in the boat, an idea prevailed that it must be a ship's yawl, which perhaps was washed away from the davits in a gale of wind. Nevertheless, Captain Lamark very properly determined to pass as closely to it as possible, and slacken sail, that he might inspect it more thoroughly. Accordingly, the courses were hauled up, and the top-gallant sails settled down on the caps.

This was hardly done, when a man's hat was seen to rise slowly above the gunwale of the boat, and be gently waved, while the man himself could not be seen. The sensation among the crew of the Rosamond, caused by this action, can hardly be conceived. The feeble wave of the hat, by the hardly uplifted hand, told a thrilling tale of long suffering, starvation, and helplessness.

"Mr. Hawkins," said Captain Lamark, "take a couple of hands and clear away the stern-boat, and get it all ready to be lowered. And stand by, men, to lay the main topsail to the mast."

In a few minutes the ship's progress through the water was stopped, and the fugitive boat was under the lee but a few fathoms distant. At this moment, a human head was lifted above the gunwale, and a human countenance was exhibited, at the sight of which every man shuddered with horror. The features were ghastly pale, wrinkled, almost fleshless, and distorted with agony; the eyes were preternaturally large, bloodshot, and glaring, giving an expression to the features which seemed the very incarnation of despair and insanity.

As the ship was slowly surging past, Mr. Digges threw a rope into the boat, and told the man to lay hold of it; but the wretched being was too weak to make the slightest effort for the preservation of his life. A moment afterwards, and Mr. Hawkins was alongside the boat in the ship's yawl. He found it half full of water, and the dead body of a man in a sailor's dress was washing about in the bottom of the boat, while the miserable object which had exhibited signs of life,

13*

reclining on the after-thwart, in vain attempted to speak, but could only indicate by signs that his throat was too parched to utter an articulate sound.

With great care and no little difficulty, Mr. Hawkins succeeded in transferring the living skeleton to the yawl, and in a few minutes he was conveyed to the ship; passed up the gangway, and safely landed on the quarter-deck. Restoratives were promptly administered, and small quantities of nourishing food; and under the judicious management of Captain Lamark, the poor suffering sailor, who, when fallen in with, seemed in the very last extremity, gradually recovered his health. Some days, however, elapsed before he was able to give a connected sketch of the circumstances which brought him to the unhappy condition from which he was so providentially rescued.

It appeared, from his account, that his name was James Maltby, and that he belonged to an English brig lying at anchor in Table Bay. One Sunday afternoon, Maltby and a shipmate named Edward Cope obtained leave of the mate to go ashore in the small boat, on condition of returning in the course of an hour. But on shore they fell in with some jovial companions, freely partook of the intoxicating cup, forgot their promise to the mate, and abandoned themselves to dissipation.

The approaching darkness, however, reminded them of their neglect of duty, and they staggered down towards the jetty, and entered the boat with the intention of going on board the brig. Cope, however, was too far gone to pull an oar, and stretching himself in the bottom of the boat, soon fell asleep. Maltby then thrust his oar over the stern and began to scull, but making a false movement, he lost overboard his oar. He then relinquished all further efforts to reach the brig, and followed the example of his companion. The boat drifted out to sea, and on awakening to a sense of their condition, the next morning, the two men found themselves eight or ten miles from the land, with the wind off shore, without sails or a scrap of provisions, and with only one oar to aid them in returning to Table. Bay. They continued in sight of the high mountains about the cape for two days, but on the morning of the third day found themselves in the midst of the South Atlantic Ocean, no land in sight, destitute of food or drink, without a compass, and drifting about at the mercy of the winds and waves.

This was only the beginning of their sufferings, which were soon greater than one would suppose human nature could bear. Once or twice they caught a little water, when it rained, in the bottom of the boat; but it was so mixed with salt water, that it tended rather to increase than assuage their thirst. After having been five days on the water, and meeting with no vessel, they gave up all hope, and resolved to meet, with due resignation, the dreadful death that seemed inevitable, comforting themselves with the reflection that the boat would probably be picked up, and their dead bodies prove that they did not wilfully desert from their vessel. They pledged themselves to each other by the most solemn oaths, that if one died before the other, the survivor would not feast on the body of his shipmate.

Another day passed, when the boat, which had hitherto proved staunch, sprung aleak, and Maltby made an effort to bale out the water with his hat. But Cope gave himself up to despair; his reason at length deserted him; cramps seized his limbs; he was the picture of famine, the prey of a devouring fever; his mouth foamed, his tongue was swollen to a frightful size, and his eyes lost all their brilliancy. On the seventh day, Cope made a convulsive effort to throw himself out of the boat, and was with difficulty prevented by Maltby. He then sunk down beneath the thwarts and expired.

Maltby had not strength enough to remove the dead body of his shipmate, or even to bale out the boat, but remained in one position in the stern-sheets, leaning against the after-thwart, until the following day, in full possession of his senses, however, and mentally praying to God to relieve him from his sufferings, and forgive his sins; and on the eighth day after having been driven out to sea, and twenty-six hours after his shipmate had breathed his last, he lifted his eyes, his head being even with the gunwale, and saw a ship heading towards him. His heart, which had almost ceased to beat, fluttered with a feeling of hope. He was unable to rise, but he lifted his hat and feebly waved it as a signal.

A heavy penalty did these two men pay for indulging in intemperate habits. Maltby declared that he had learned a lesson which would be of priceless value to him through life. And it is to be hoped that he religiously kept his promise, that he would ever after abstain from all intoxicating drinks.

That night, in the middle watch, Mark Rowland, while walking the deck with Mr. Hawkins, gave utterance to the thoughts that were uppermost in his mind connected with the adventure of the previous day, and made eager inquiries of that worthy officer if he had ever met with a case of the kind in his long experience at sea.

"Such cases are by no means uncommon, Mark," said Mr. Hawkins. "Boats and small vessels are sometimes driven out of harbors and away from coasts, when they are al-together unprepared for such a misfortune. But if not swamped in the gale which sent them adrift, they are usu-ally picked up before the men undergo much suffering. I never met with but one case of the kind, and that was an exception to the general rule. The vessel, for it was not a boat, had been drifting about more than six months before it was picked up."

"Six months!" cried Mark; "and were there men on board of her during the whole of that time?"

"Certainly. I'll tell you how it happened. I once made a voyage from Boston to San Francisco in the ship Mandril, after a cargo of hides. In the Pacific Ocean, not far from the coast, in latitude of about forty degrees, we fell in with a Japanese junk, with three men on board, who were in a truly distressed condition. I was one of the men who went with the officer to examine the wreck.

"The state of affairs on board looked dark and gloomy enough. The junk was only about thirty tons burden, and had on board part of a cargo of rice, a large portion of which had been soaked in the salt water and spoiled. She was covered with barnacles of monstrous size, and a sort of clams from two to five inches in length. Her masts had been carried away by the deck; her rudder was also gone; she leaked badly; and ropes had been strapped around and around her to keep her from foundering. There was little else on board excepting the rice in the hold, and a few articles belonging to the men. There were in a cask a few gallons of rain water, that had been caught in a shower, but no food of any description, besides the rice, excepting a few strips of shark they had lately caught, and which showed strong symptoms of decay. Nevertheless, the men who constituted her crew seemed in pretty good health, and able to do good service at the pump; otherwise she must have gone down long before we fell in with her.

"We took from her half a dozen bags of the best rice, a few pieces of rope, the three men, who rejoiced exceedingly at being rescued from the sinking wreck, and returned to the ship. The junk could not have remained above water four-and-twenty hours longer. Her bottom seemed to be coming to pieces.

"It appeared from facts that have since been ascertained,

that this vessel was a coasting junk, and had been blown off
the coast and dismasted in one of those typhoons which are
so terribly destructive in those seas.   Knowing nothing of
navigation or the effects of currents and winds, without
even a compass, and destitute of masts or sails, these unfortunate Japanese sailors were unable to make any exertions
for their safety, excepting to keep their frail bark afloat.
The heavy gales from the westward and currents had drifted
them to the eastward, inasmuch that, while they remained
in nearly the same parallel of latitude, they were driven
about twenty-four hundred miles in *one hundred and ninety
days!* There was no mistake in this, for one of the men,
who acted as skipper, kept a journal from the time he lost
sight of the land, until fallen in with by the Mandril.

"I never saw gratitude displayed with greater warmth
and sincerity than by these poor fellows.   On our way home
we landed them at Coquimbo, whence, I since learned, they
managed after a while to find means of returning to their
own country."

CHAPTER XIII.

Soon after the ship Rosamond saved poor Maltby from a terrible death, a heavy easterly gale commenced, which lasted for several days. When the gale subsided, the high mountains on the Cape of Good Hope were in sight; and on the following day the ship entered the harbor and anchored in Table Bay.

From the anchorage in this remarkable bay, Mark Rowland beheld a wide and varied, a novel and deeply interesting scene. There were, as it appeared, spread out before him the many vessels of different nations and characters at anchor in the bay, and others discharging or taking in cargoes at the quays; the city of Cape Town itself, with its flat-roofed, white or ruddy-colored houses, and its numerous towers and spires; the neat villas and straw-colored cottages stretching along back of the city, and peeping through the dense foliage; the grim batteries on the Lion's Rump, a short distance from the sea; on each side of the city, the lofty crags known as the Devil's Peak and the Lion's Head; and directly back of Cape Town the long, lofty, flat-topped Table Mountain itself, destitute of vegetation, and rising to a height of thirty-six hundred feet above the level of the sea.

Nor were Mark's astonishment and admiration less when he landed, and traversed the streets of that old Dutch city, and saw the different kinds of people, and especially the

many varieties of the African race, who were actively engaged in their wonted occupations. He saw there the genuine Hottentot, with his sooty skin, his long heels, and his
protruding lips ; the Bushman, with his low forehead and
expressionless visage, and the fierce-looking Caffre, with his
glittering eye and savage demeanor. He also met with several unadulterated descendants of the old Dutch Boers,
more appropriately called Boors, the original settlers of the
Cape, with their heavy frames, stolid countenances, coarse
habits, and unprepossessing manners, freezing at the foun-
tain every gush of social intercourse.

Mark Rowland did not go far enough beyond the town to
encounter, in their wild state, lions, rhinoceroses, hippopota-
muses, antelopes, camelopards, elephants, pythons, or even
the mischievous, vindictive, tailless, and hideous-looking bab-
boons, which are often seen in herds in the vicinity of Table
Mountain, and all of which are described with great gusto
by veracious travellers, to the great delight of wonder-lov-
ing and voracious readers. He saw, however, in Cape Town
itself, many specimens of wild animals altogether new to
him, which had been " caught, cribbed, and confined," and
exhibited for show or for sale. Indeed, he saw enough to
give him an exalted opinion of and a considerable insight
into the interesting subject of natural history.

Mark had read in one of his school-books an account of a
heroic act of an inhabitant of Cape Town in saving the
lives of men belonging to a vessel that was shipwrecked in
the Roads. He inquired into the facts, and found they were
all true as related by Sparrman, a celebrated traveller and
voyageur in the last century.

The incident occurred in 1775, but will never be forgotten
by the admirers of courage and benevolence. A Dutch ship
named the Jong Thomas was at anchor in the bay during
the inclement season, when a violent storm suddenly com-

menced, and the heavy waves rushing in from the ocean forced the ship from her anchors, and she was driven ashore on the north side of the bay, some distance from the beach. The cries of the mariners were distinctly heard; but the sea washed over the ship with such fury that no boat could live, and some who attempted to swim ashore were dashed to pieces on the rocks, or carried back by the refluent wave and drowned.

The ship was driven ashore soon after daylight in the morning, and intelligence was immediately conveyed to the government house, when a small military force was promptly dispatched to the seaside, not so much to assist in saving life as to prevent the pillage of such portions of the cargo as might be washed ashore. It happened that one of the keepers of the Dutch East India Company's menagerie, whose name was Voltemad, rode out of the town on a large and spirited horse to carry breakfast to his son, who was a corporal in the company stationed on the beach. He was thus an early witness to the distressing scene, and, moved by a generous compassion, though he could not swim, he fixed himself firmly on his noble horse and swam him off to the ship. Telling some of the crew to lay. hold of a rope which he threw to them, and others to grasp the tail of his horse, he turned about and carried them safely to the shore. In this way he made several trips, and saved a considerable number of lives.

At last this bold and generous man fell a victim to his philanthropy. His horse becoming fatigued with such unusual exertions, he waited a while on the beach for the animal to rest. But, stimulated by the cries and prayers of the unfortunate men on board the ship, he hastened to their relief before the horse had sufficiently renewed his strength. It also happened, unfortunately, that too many sought to be saved at the same time, and the poor animal, with his bold

14

rider and the hapless mariners, who were clinging to the trappings of the horse, all sunk, and were seen no more.

The East India Directors in Holland seem to have appreciated the noble conduct of Voltemad.   On receiving intelligence of the affair, they ordered one of their ships to be called after his name, and the story of his humanity to be inscribed on its stern. They further did honor to themselves by enjoining their agents at the Cape to provide for the descendants of Voltemad, in case there were any such, and put them in a way of speedily and effectually making their fortunes. They also ordered a monument to be erected to the memory of this self-devoted philanthropist.

Unfortunately for the young corporal, who was the only child of Voltemad, the agents of the Company in the southern hemisphere did not cherish the same sentiments of gratitude.   This young man, who had been a looker-on while his father sacrificed himself in the service of the Company and of mankind, made an application for the place which his father had held in the menagerie, humble as it was. *His application was refused!* Stung by the disappointment, he immediately left the Cape of Good Hope, and went to Batavia, hoping to find better fortunes among a more generous people. Here he was attacked by the malignant fever incidental to the climate, and died before the news of the acknowledgment of his father's services, and the kind feelings of the Company towards himself, could reach him. This is not a solitary instance where an act of god-like humanity has gone unrequited by an unfeeling world.

On the day on which the last portion of the cargo of the Rosamond was discharged, Mr. Digges took it into his wise head to make a great display, astonish the crews of the foreign ships in the harbor, and let them know that an American " can do some things as well as others."

Preparations were made accordingly. A big gun, charged

with a double allowance of powder, was to be fired; at which signal the American ensign was to be hoisted at the spanker peak, the flaunting burgee, with the eagle and stars, at the mizzen sky-sail masthead, the pennant at the main, and the American jack at the fore; and at the same moment the *last bale of goods* was to be hoisted out of the hold, and run up to the main yard-arm.

The arrangements were completed. Every man was at his station, and Mr. Digges, in high glee, standing on the quarter-deck with the trumpet to his mouth, in a Stentor-like tone, gave the word, " FIRE."

The gun spoke in a voice like thunder, which, of course, made the Rosamond the observed of all observers; the flags were all displayed, and the last bale hoisted out agreeably to the programme, and, to the great admiration of all the foreigners in the port, who could hardly understand what Brother Jonathan would be at.

It so happened that at this time there was a little Pariah dog on board, named Trip, — a timid, harmless, inoffensive animal, a great favorite with the captain. Little Trip was standing near the gun-carriage at the forward part of the main deck, attentively watching the operations, and apparently wondering at what was going on, but without having the slightest suspicion of the stunning report which was about to salute his ears. When the gun was fired, the shock came upon him with terrible effect. It actually knocked him over, and deprived him of his wits. He uttered a mournful howl, sprang to his feet, and ran aft the whole length of the deck, with the fleetness of a greyhound, jumped on the taff-rail, and, turning his head for a second, gave a terrified look behind him; then, as if eager to escape from the clutches of some imaginary monster, jumped ten or fifteen feet over the stern into the water, and was never seen afterwards.

Captain Lamark, on being informed of the fate of his

favorite dog, through an ill-timed desire on the part of Mr. Digges to startle the good people in Cape Town and Table Bay, and make a noise in the world, was quite angry. He severely reprimanded that officer for indulging such ambitious impulses, and never heartily forgave him for having made such a fool of himself, as he termed it, and been the cause of the death of poor Trip.

Captain Lamark, finding some difficulty in procuring the articles of merchandise he was in quest of, the Rosamond was detained two months at the Cape. Urged by the promptings of a generous nature, the captain acted as Mark's agent in managing and investing the treasure which our hero found in the island of St. Paul. He regarded this as a sacred trust, and purchased on Mark's account a quantity of wool, wines, and hides, which he put on board the ship, exacting, of course, a fair freight, and assuring Mark that he would derive a good profit on the goods on arriving at Boston.

On leaving the Cape, Mark Rowland took with him a goat, with a grave face, long curved horns, and a bushy beard, whose playful ways and intelligence he was greatly charmed with, and which he intended as a gift to his sister Ellen, if he should be so fortunate as ever to reach his home in Glenmaple. And greatly did he rejoice when the sailors, with the jovial song of " Yeo heave O," handled their handspikes, and lifted the ponderous anchor from its briny resting-place; and the good old ship Rosamond, to which by this time he had become greatly attached, with a fine breeze and a large spread of canvas, sailed majestically out of Table Bay, the remarkable mountain, with its level summit, every minute lessening in the distance, and in a few hours vanishing from his sight.

And now, fairly embarked in a strong ship, with a favorable wind, after meeting with adventures which had developed his energies, and would remain indelibly impressed on his memory for life, the thoughts of home took complete possession of his mind. His mother! His kind, indulgent, ever affectionate mother! who was so unwilling that he should leave his home, and brave the dangers of the seas! How had she borne his long absence? Had she heard of his being left on the island of St. Paul? Had she given him up for lost, and sunk under the blow? Had she found friends to console her in affliction, and relieve the sufferings of ill-health and poverty?

On the passage home, Mark Rowland could fully sympathize with the unamiable feelings of the captain and crew, when the wind, after baffling about for a time, fixed itself in the very quarter to which they wished to steer; or, what was still more annoying, died away, and a dead calm prevailed, which threatened to last for days. At such a time Mark could appreciate the sentiment contained in the following lines by the poet Fields: —

> " A welcome to the rushing blast
>   That stirs the waters now.
> Ye white-plum'd heralds of the deep,
>   Make music round her prow.
> Give sea-room to the roaring gale;
>   Let stormy trumpets blow;
> *But chain ten thousand fathoms-down*
>   *The sluggish calm below.*"

Captain Lamark, after leaving the Cape of Good Hope, was desirous of getting to the southward into the region of the trade-winds, as rapidly as possible. But the winds came from the northward, with boisterous weather, and the ship's progress was slow, averaging not more than a degree each day for a week, until in the latitude of twenty-seven and a half degrees she fell in with the regular "south-east trades," which wafted her steadily along on her way, until she nearly reached the equator.

Ships bound home from the Cape of Good Hope, or ports beyond it in the Indian Seas, find this part of their passage particularly delightful. The wind, although often moderate, remains fixed in one point, and the ship ploughs her way through a smooth sea, directly before it, with royals, sky-sails, and "studding-sails both sides, alow and aloft." There is no fear of squalls or sudden changes. The air is balmy and the temperature delicious. This is indeed the very poetry of navigation. " If such winds and weather were always met with at sea," said Mr. Hawkins to Mark Rowland, " sailors might hang up their marline-spikes, and let the old women sail and navigate the ships."

As the island of Ascension lay almost directly in the route of the Rosamond towards the equator, Captain La-mark thought he would endeavor to get a sight of it in order to test the accuracy of his chronometer and sextant; and one day, having ascertained his precise latitude at twelve o'clock, on the passage of the sun across the meridian, he said that if his instruments for determining the longitude were correct, the island of Ascension ought soon to be in sight, as Green Mountain, the highest part of the island, could be seen from a long distance, and the island was sit-uated in a parallel of latitude only thirty-five miles to the northward of the ship, the latitude of the ship being in seven degrees and twenty-two minutes south.

Acting upon this hint, Mark Rowland sprang into the fore-rigging like a squirrel, and climbed upwards and up-wards until he reached the fore-royal mast-head, and no sooner had he cast his eyes around the horizon than he cried out, " Land ho! about three points on the starboard bow!"

He could only see the faint outline of the upper part of Green Mountain. But the mountain could not be seen from the deck until nearly an hour afterwards. Captain Lamark felt greatly pleased at having made such a capital land-fall, giving assurance of the accuracy of his instruments and his skill in their management.

As the Rosamond had so recently left port, and was well supplied with the various articles which are supposed to make a sailor's life not only endurable but comfortable, Captain Lamark did not think it worth while to anchor, but altering the ship's course a couple of points, passed along within about a mile of the island, which they reached by five o'clock in the afternoon, and obtained a fine view of its general character and appearance.

In answer to the many questions which Mark Rowland put to Captain Lamark, who, in a passage from Manilla some years before, had actually landed on the island of Ascension, that gentleman gave Mark the following information.

" The island of Ascension is a huge, volcanic mass of rocks thrown up from the bottom of the ocean. It is about twenty miles in circumference, and its bleak and barren appearance, when seen from the water, does not belie the reality. It is a rough, rocky, uneven spot, with but little soil, no trees, and scanty vegetation of any kind. The highest point of the island is three thousand feet above the level of the sea. Goats and rats are about the only quadrupeds which are found on the island in a wild state. It has been held by Great Britain as a military post, ever since Napoleon Bonaparte was gratuitously furnished with lodgings at St. Helena by the British Government. Vessels which touch there are supplied with water, sometimes with vegetables of a very ordinary quality, and turtles in abundance. These turtles are large, and furnish delicate and nutritious food, and are heartily welcomed on board ships, which having been long at sea, are deficient in fresh provisions.

There is little else to gratify the curiosity of the traveller, or satisfy the longings of the naturalist."

Mark Rowland had often heard these famous turtles spoken of and described by the officers and men of the Rosamond, and was very anxious to see what kind of looking animals they were. And in a few days after the ship passed the island of Ascension, he met with an opportunity not only to *see* one of these queer, uncouth-looking animals, but to be convinced of their existence by *tangible* proof.

After the ship had crossed the equator, and was making the best of her way through the region of calms, showers, and thunder-squalls, before reaching the latitude of the north-east trade-winds, a dark object was seen one forenoon on the water by the man at the wheel. He pointed it out to Mr. Digges, who was officer of the deck at the time. That officer recognized it once as a turtle — as a turtle of uncommon size — asleep on the water!

It was nearly calm at the time. The ship barely had steerage-way. There was no prospect of a breeze, and although heavy clouds hung about the horizon, it would be long before they could reach the zenith. Mr. Digges was an epicure in his way, and professed to be inordinately fond of turtle; and the sight of the animal quietly reposing on the water, unconscious of danger, conjured up rapturous visions of delicious turtle steaks, and unctuous soups and fricassees, such as would bewilder, captivate, and charm the palate of the most fastidious epicure. Thrusting his head down the companion-way, " Captain Lamark," said that trustworthy officer, " there is a fine turtle asleep on the water, but a short distance off; shall I lower away the jolly-boat, nab him, and bring him on board?"

"That is more easily said than done," replied the captain. "It is as hard to catch a turtle asleep as a weasel. I have no objection to your making the trial, but you had better take the grainse with you, and strike a prong through one of his flippers, if you want to make sure of him."

Mr. Digges was one of those men who seldom take proffered advice, or adopt the suggestions of others, and who, in consequence, are often involved in trouble. "I want no grainse," said he, turning towards Mr. Hawkins, "or anything of the kind, to catch a sleeping turtle."

The ship's way was stopped, and Mr. Digges, Mark Rowland, and Harry Linsay, stepped into the boat. Mark had not much faith in the mate's success, after the captain's admonition, but wished to obtain as close a view of the animal as possible.

Mr. Digges, with his sleeves rolled up, bare-armed for the contest, — like Pentapolin of old, — and determination in his eye, took his station in the bow; Mark stood near him, and both fixed their eyes intently on the drowsy reptile, while Harry Linsay, agreeably to the directions of the mate, slowly and cautiously sculled the boat through the water. "So! steady as you go!" said Mr. Digges. "Don't give her too much way! Steer straight for the turtle; keep him right ahead! There, that will do! Way enough! Stand by, Mark, and if I should miss him, grab him by the flipper, and hold on like a nor'-wester to a West Indiaman in Massachusetts Bay in mid-winter!"

But the turtle, although pretending to be asleep, was in reality wide awake, or was awakened by a presentiment of coming danger. As the boat reached him, and Mr. Digges with outstretched arms made an effort to seize him, the reptile with a quick motion dodged him and darted across the bow of the boat, thus placing himself within reach of Mark Rowland. Just as he was on the point of diving, with his head down and his tail up, Mark grabbed him by the hind flipper, and shouted exultantly, "I've got him! I've got him!"

"Hold on, Mark," screamed Mr. Digges; "hold on for your life!" and he stepped over to the other side of the boat to Mark's assistance.

This turtle was an animal of monstrous size, of the loggerhead species, weighing at least two hundred and fifty pounds, and his strength in the water was prodigious. Terrified at such unceremonious and unkind treatment, the animal made a desperate struggle to get away, exerting all its muscular power, and for a brief moment it was a question whether the turtle would be captured and conveyed in triumph on board the ship, or Mark Rowland, who, stimulated by the loud cries of the mate, would not relinquish his hold, go overboard.

The struggle was a short but severe one. It was decided in favor of the turtle by Mr. Digges, himself, who on stepping to Mark's assistance gave the boat a list that upset Mark's equilibrium, already endangered by the struggles of the reptile; and *overboard he went*, still clinging like a hero to the turtle, and both disappeared beneath the waves.

The turtle was never heard of afterwards, and doubtless rejoiced exceedingly at having shaken off its pursuer, and escaped without a wound; and quite likely in its aquatic haunts it has often related for the edification of admiring audiences, the perilous adventure it once met with in the upper regions.

In a few moments Mark Rowland appeared, bouncing up to the surface like a cork, and blowing and puffing like a porpoise. He was taken into the boat, and the parties returned to the ship silent and disappointed. Indeed, Mr. Digges looked crest-fallen and cross, and exhibited a very unamiable temper for a week afterwards, and was observed to look particularly savage and wrathful, whenever the word *turtle* was mentioned in his hearing.

CHAPTER XIV.

THE goat which Mark Rowland brought on board at the Cape of Good Hope, proved to be a lively, frisky animal, playful and sometimes mischievous. And his mischievous propensities were rather encouraged than otherwise by the sailors, who regarded him with much interest and affection, and took charge of his education. They named him Samson; he had the range of the decks, and took great delight in chasing the men about when they were engaged in their various duties, and exercising his skill in *butting*, an accomplishment in which he had received no little encouragement and instruction from the sailors, and in which he showed himself an apt scholar. Indeed, not having judgment enough to select the proper times, places, and persons, when, where, and on whom, to test his force and adroitness in that peculiar and effective mode of attack, he more than once involved himself in trouble.

Mr. Digges was a good officer, scrupulously attentive to his duties. He was somewhat stout-built, had a bald head, and but little fun in his disposition. He never joked, and seldom laughed at the jokes of others. Such men are, perhaps, well enough in their way, for the sake of variety; but it is well for the happiness of mankind that there are not many of them.

Mr. Digges took a dislike to Samson when he was first brought on board; and grumbled without stint at the cap-

tain's folly, in thus allowing a four-legged beast to cumber
the ship, clutter up the decks, and be always in the way.
He could never get reconciled to the presence of Samson,
but took every opportunity to give him a kick, or indulge
his hatred in a manner equally unjustifiable. Samson bore
this ill-treatment for some time without resistance or even
remonstrance; but at last an opportunity offered for retalia-
tion, which the mate little anticipated, but which Samson
knowingly or unwittingly improved to its fullest extent; and
thus " the whirligig of time brought about its revenges."

It was the Sabbath day. The ship was just emerging
from the tropics. The weather was pleasant and warm, with
a moderate breeze nearly abeam. After a hearty dinner the
captain had retired to his state-room, and was indulging in a
nap, and Mr. Hawkins, the second mate, had followed the
captain's laudable example. Mr. Digges, whose watch was
on deck, after taking a few turns fore and aft, thought that
instead of reading a chapter or two in the Bible, as he should
have done, he would improve his leisure time in washing a
few of his garments, which he easily persuaded himself was
an act of *necessity*.

Accordingly, having clandestinely provided himself with a
bucket of fresh water, Mr. Digges took his station in the lee
scuppers, and made due preparations for business. The
weather being warm, he threw off his hat and jacket, and
rolling up his shirt sleeves, and stooping down over the
bucket, in a posture resembling the natural attitude of a
quadruped, he went briskly to work.

At this critical moment Samson came from the forecastle,
having been reciting some practical lessons in butting, for
the amusement of the sailors. He saw the mate in a stooping posture, with his shiny cranium bobbing up and down,
and taking it for a challenge to a trial of strength and skill,
and possibly influenced by shadowy visions of ill-treatment,

which flitted before his mind's eye, he stepped back a pace or two, to allow space for a good run, and raising his head for a correct aim, rushed with the force of a rock from a ballista full against the bald head which was nodding defiance.

The shock was a tremendous one, and could be heard all over the ship. The unfortunate mate, who little dreamed of such an encounter, was knocked over backwards, and fell sprawling and senseless in the scuppers, and his cranium was saved from fracture only by the unusual thickness of his skull.

Samson escaped "death or worse punishment," only by the unconsciousness of his opponent, who was borne into the cabin, where his head was bound up, and he was restored to his senses. But his rage at such an unprovoked attack knew no bounds. He vowed all sorts of vengeance against the goat, and was hardly restrained by the captain's authority from giving the animal a good rope's-ending, and then knocking him in the head.

A week or two after this occurrence, which furnished a fruitful theme for conversation among all hands, and tended to enliven the ship's company, the ship Rosamond entered the Gulf Stream, and met with rough weather. A gale came on suddenly in squalls, and about six bells in the middle watch all hands were called to reef top-sails. It was dark and rainy; heavy black clouds rose from the horizon, and passed rapidly over the zenith, while the sea, suddenly agitated by a change of wind, spitefully tossed volumes of spray over the decks.

The top-sail halliards were let go, and the yards clued down for reefing; the main-sail was hauled up, the spanker lowered, and the jib hauled down. The men went aloft and took a double reef in the top-sails, but, in coming down from the foretop-sail yard, one of the men, Jack Radkin,

15

was startled by the sight of a strange-looking object, which seemed to be clinging to the lee foretop-mast backstays, just above the level of the foretop, and kicking out its legs like a jumping jack.

Radkin hailed it, thinking it might be one of his shipmates, amusing himself in that strange manner, but received no answer. The darkness prevented his analyzing its shape or character, but he saw enough to arouse all his fears, and convince him that some terrible calamity was impending over the ship. He slid down on deck by the first rope he could catch, at the risk of breaking his neck.

" Mr. Digges! Mr. Digges!" he shouted, as soon as he reached the deck; " Davy Jones is aloft, and holding on to the lee backstays!"

" Don't be a natural-born fool, Jack! What do you mean?"

" He is *there*, sir! Davy Jones is *there*, sir," said Jack, with a voice tremulous with terror, pointing aloft; " horns and all! I saw him, as I came down, as plain as the nose on my face. I almost touched him. You may see him now, sir. He is ten shades blacker than the pitchy darkness that is around us."

On looking aloft, this strange announcement received a terrible confirmation by the appearance of a dark, undefined object in the direction indicated by Jack Radkin. A panic seized the ship's company, which was increased, when, on counting noses, not a man was missing from deck. The captain was known to be snug in his berth in the cabin, and Snowball, the cook, was lending a hand on deck. Yet *somebody* was aloft; that was clear. It could be none of the ship's company, and therefore the conclusion was inevitable : it must be the great enemy of mankind, or one of his agents, on some fearful mission.

Mr. Hawkins, and one or two of the most intrepid sailors,

went half-way up the lee fore-rigging, to obtain a more distinct glimpse of the object which had excited such alarm; but a nearer view only served to confirm the fears already entertained. Bob Randy, a bold, reckless reprobate, on being urged by Mr. Digges to go up higher, and "cut the critter loose," whatever it was, and throw it overboard, refused, declaring that he feared nothing in the shape of a living man, but as for fighting a black, horned demon, there was no such obligation in the shipping articles.

By this time the squall had subsided, the clouds had become broken, and objects could be seen more distinctly. Mr. Digges now summoned all his courage to his aid, and, with a degree of daring which reflected great credit on the character of that active officer, determined to go aloft himself, and ascertain, from personal inspection, the nature of the mysterious phantom which had frightened the whole ship's company. His compressed lips and scowling countenance marked his unshaken resolution, as he ascended the lee fore-rigging, cautiously passed over the rattlings, keeping a good look-out above his head, until he reached the futtock shrouds. Here, pausing in his career, he took a good look at the monster.

"Do you see him?" inquired the second mate, in a low voice, as he stood on the gunwale, looking up.

"See him? To be sure I do," replied Mr. Digges.

"What does he look like?" asked Mr. Hawkins.

"He looks like Davy Jones, and nobody else," said Mr. Digges, with a shudder. "I can see his horns! I can see his tail! I can see his cloven foot! I can see his long beard! and — *dowse my glim, if it isn't that confounded goat, Samson, strung up by the gills like a stock-fish, after all!*"

Mr. Digges came down quicker than he went up. He told Mr. Hawkins to set the sails and trim the yards, and walked

off without saying another word.   Soon afterwards he went
below, highly mortified, indignant, and disgusted.

The key thus furnished, the mystery was soon unlocked.
Samson was found to be actually hanging and dangling in
mid-air.   It was subsequently ascertained that, when the jib
halliards were let go by the run, and the jib hauled down,
the goat must have been standing around, as usual, to see
what was going on, and had stepped into the coil of the
rope just as it was thrown on deck.   When the halliards
were let go, a couple of turns of the rope caught him around
the neck, and, in spite of his struggles and resistance, carried him aloft.   Thus, without any intention on the part of
the goat, or any of the ship's company, poor Samson paid
the penalty for being where he was not wanted, and was
" hanged by the neck until he was dead."

Captain Lamark was a skilful navigator.   He not only had
a good chronometer and a good sextant, and knew how to
use them, but he was gifted with a sound judgment, and,
even in the absence of the sun, moon, and stars, if " dead
reckoning " was to be relied on, he would be at all times
aware of the exact position of the ship.   He placed, however, but little confidence in dead reckoning.   He regarded
it at best but a rough kind of guess-work.   On approaching
a coast in cloudy weather, when neither the longitude nor
latitude could be ascertained by observation, he relied altogether on his *lead and line*.   He often said that if soundings were resorted to on approaching the land, and the lead
frequently used, shipwrecks would be reduced at least fifty
per centum; for there were very few parts of the ocean
where the soundings would not indicate, in a manner which
could not be misunderstood, the proximity of danger.

After leaving the Gulf Stream, Captain Lamark steered a
course to the northward, intending to pass through the South
Channel: that is, the wide and safe passage between the

shoals of Nantucket on the west, and St. George's Bank on the east. He always had a horror of the Vineyard Sound, with its Holmes Hole, extra charges for pilotage and ship's stores, besides a tedious detention of weeks or months.

On approaching the entrance of the South Channel, the weather was mild and the atmosphere foggy. The captain had taken no observation for the previous twenty-four hours, and, with the currents which prevail in that quarter, and light and baffling winds, he was by no means certain of the position of the ship. Nevertheless, he kept on fearlessly, depending on the lead, feeling assured that it would not only give him seasonable warning of his approach to the land, but also indicate, by the character of the soundings, which side of the channel he was approaching, and thus enable him to steer a correct course.

Night came on; it was quite dark, drizzly, and foggy. No object, not even the light in a lighthouse, could be seen at the distance of two ship's lengths from the jib-boom. There was now a steady breeze from the south-east, but the ship, although under full sail, was in good working trim. Captain Lamark was on deck, for at a time like this, he would trust to the vigilance of no one but himself. The lead was thrown from time to time, and the soundings carefully noted; twenty, twenty-five, and thirty fathoms, — sand, or sand and shells.

At four bells in the first watch (ten o'clock), all hands being on deck, the captain remarked to his officers, " Surely, we ought to be as far along as the south shoal of Nantucket by this time. These numerous tide-rips, almost amounting to breakers, are sure indications that shoal water is not far off. Take another cast of the lead."

The lead was thrown, and conveyed the intelligence that the ship was in fifteen fathoms of water. A few minutes

15*

afterwards, the water had shoaled to eight fathoms, rocky bottom.

"Starboard your helm," said Captain Lamark to the man at the wheel; "I know where we are now. We are on the tail of St. George's shoal. Brail up the spanker and square the yards. Keep her west-north-west."

"Aye, aye, sir," responded the helmsman. "West-north-west it is."

The water soon deepened, and in fifteen minutes no soundings could be obtained with fifty fathoms of line. "Hurrah!" exclaimed the captain; "'tis all right! Hey for Cape Cod! If the wind holds, and the fog clears away, we shall make the highlands of the cape by noon to-morrow."

Notwithstanding Captain Lamark was so confident that he knew the exact position of his ship, he caused the lead to be thrown at short intervals through the night. "It is barely *possible* that I may be mistaken," he remarked to his officers, "and it is always best to be on the safe side."

Mr. Digges thought the captain was over-cautious, and that such constant heaving of the lead was a very troublesome operation, and altogether unnecessary. But he wisely refrained from expressing his discontented feelings in the hearing of the captain.

Mr. Hawkins, however, took a different view of the matter, and not only obeyed the orders of the captain with alacrity and cheerfulness, but anticipated his wishes in regard to the soundings.

In the middle watch, while the captain had gone below to obtain a little sleep, being weary and worn out with care and watchfulness, Mr. Hawkins took occasion to express to Mark Rowland his admiration of the conduct of Captain Lamark when approaching the coast. "If every captain," said Mr. Hawkins, "were as prudent as Captain Lamark, many a strong ship would have been saved from shipwreck, and many a brave and faithful sailor would have been saved from a sudden death.

"I was once," continued Mr. Hawkins, warming with his subject, "before the mast in the ship Redondo, Captain Lanrock, bound from Liverpool to New York, with a heavy and valuable cargo. The captain was a worthy man, a good sailor, and a skilful navigator. But he liked his ease ; he could not bear to be deprived of his usual amount of sleep, and reposed a great deal more confidence in the fidelity and vigilance of his officers than they deserved. After a long and tedious passage of fifty-six days, for the Redondo was a heavy sailer, we made, just at night, the Jersey coast, some ten or fifteen miles to the southward of the highlands of Navesink. The wind was to the northward, and there was a heavy sea running, and as we could not obtain a pilot, the captain concluded to stand off and on during the night, hoping to find himself off Sandy Hook in the morning.

"At five o'clock we were well in with the land, in fifteen fathoms of water. We then tacked ship and stood off to the eastward until eight o'clock, when, with a light breeze, we again tacked and stood in shore. The chief mate, Mr. Gargin, whom the captain believed to be true and trustworthy, but who would steal a nap on deck whenever he had a chance, aye, even sleep with his head in a bucket of water, had charge of the first watch.

"The captain told Mr. Gargin to keep a good lookout, and take a cast of the lead every fifteen minutes at least, and at four bells (ten o'clock) put the ship round with her head off shore ; and if at any time he found less than fifteen fathoms, to tack ship immediately. 'And, Mr. Gargin,' continued he, 'if there should be any change in the wind or weather, give me a call ; and be sure to call me at twelve o'clock.'

"'Aye, aye, sir!' responded Mr. Gargin, somewhat gruffly.

"Captain Lanrock went below, feeling satisfied that he had done *his* duty. He unrigged himself and turned into his berth, as unconcernedly as if he had taken lodgings at a first-class hotel, throwing off with his coat all responsibility for the fate of the ship and crew.

"He had hardly closed his eyes before the wind hauled a couple of points to the eastward, and rapidly increased to a strong breeze. The weather also became thick and rainy, and the ship now dashed on towards the shore with nearly double the speed with which she left it a short time before. The mate, warmly wrapped in his monkey-jacket, which might very properly be called a *waprascal*, after taking a a few turns fore and aft, seated himself on the weather hen-coop, gradually assumed a recumbent position, and was soon lost to sense and motion.

"Mr. Gargin was aroused out of his nap by the helmsman when he announced that it was ten o'clock. The mate shook himself, looked around, and ordered the lead to be thrown. It was ascertained that the ship was in eighteen fathoms of water.

"'All right!' said Mr. Gargin. 'If she keeps in eighteen fathoms she will never go ashore.'

"'That's as true as if Old Neptune himself had said it,' remarked old Ben Lufkin, who had just taken the wheel.

"'We will stand on for half an hour longer,' soliloquized the mate, 'and then we can afford to take a good stretch off.' And he threw himself down on the hen-coop again, and slept as soundly as the captain in the cabin.

"His half hour was a long one. An hour and a half passed by, and the ship meanwhile was rushing towards the land at the rate of six or seven knots through the water, aided by a heavy sea tumbling in from the eastward, and perhaps also by a strong current setting in the same direction.

"I was in the chief mate's watch, and the opinion was freely expressed among my watch-mates that we were getting too near the land for our comfort or safety. But Caleb Benson, a sort of boatswain on board, dryly remarked, 'That's no business of ours, boys! If the ship is lost, it will not be our fault. If any one of us should advise the mate to tack ship and stand off, he would receive more abuse than thanks; more kicks than coppers. By all means let matters take their own course, and we shall soon find out what that will be.'

"And soon, too soon, the crisis came. All at once was heard a loud, sullen roar, which soon died away. But the origin of that roar could not be mistaken by any one who had ever heard it. Caleb Benson shouted with a voice that could be heard all over the ship, 'BREAKERS AHEAD!' At the same moment Ben Lufkin called to the mate in a tone of great alarm, 'Mr. Gargin! Mr. Gargin! there's breakers ahead, as sure as there's sharks in the sea!'

"Mr. Gargin sprang to his feet, and was wide awake in an instant. At the same moment Captain Lanrock, hearing the cry of 'breakers!' rushed up on deck, clad only in a single garment.

"'What is the meaning of this, Mr. Gargin?' screamed the captain. 'You sleepy-headed scoundrel, you have neglected your duty, and we are lost!' At the same time he gave the mate a blow with his fist which knocked that officer headlong into the lee scuppers, and that was the last ever seen of him.

"'Hard down your helm, and stand by for stays!' shouted the captain, in a loud voice, which nevertheless could hardly be heard above the roar of the breakers, which were fearfully near.

"And even at that critical moment if the ship had worked

well, and come round, we might have filled on the other tack
and clawed off shore. But she would not ' stay,' and the
only chance was to ' wear ship.' The spanker was brailed
up, the head yards were braced round, and we boxed her
off, and got her before the wind, which by this time having
hauled into north-east, was blowing directly on shore. But
before the ship could come-to on the other tack, she was
among the breakers. She was lifted high up on the top of a
gigantic combing wave, and dashed upon the shores of the
Jersey coast, with a shock that took every man off his feet,
and shook the masts out of their steps.

" The ship swung round broadside to the wind, when a sea
came in over the quarter which swept the deck, took off the
captain, the second mate, and the helmsman, whose bodies
were afterwards picked up on the beach. The rest of us
clung to the rigging or spars as well as we could for a time ;
but how we managed to avoid being washed away at once, is
more than I know. But the ship was old and decayed, and
could not long stand this terrible pounding. She was soon
crushed like an egg-shell, and planks, timbers, spars, and
cargo were driven towards the shore. I got hold of a plank,
or a box, or a spar, I hardly know what, and determined to
cling to it as long as possible. I soon lost all sensation,
and an hour and a half afterwards found myself on the beach,
half frozen to death, and a couple of good-natured fellows
were kindly pouring whiskey down my throat to bring me to
my senses.

" Four of my shipmates were as fortunate as myself, and
reached the shore alive. All the rest of the crew perished.
This sad disaster taught me that *an officer of a ship should
never sleep in his watch on deck, or neglect to heave the lead
when approaching the land.* It also taught me that no man is
fit to command a ship, who in a critical time will trust the
property and lives for which he is responsible, to the care
and judgment of any one but himself."

CHAPTER XV.

> "Whales in the sea,
> God's voice obey."

WITH a fine breeze from the south-east, a dense and driz-zly atmosphere, and surrounded by a darkness which could almost be felt, the ship Rosamond, under snug sail, pursued her course across the South Channel towards Cape Cod, cleaving the water, and bounding along at the rate of eight or nine knots, as if anxious to get to the end of the voyage.

At midnight, the captain being still on deck, the larboard watch was roused out. When Mr. Digges came up, he remarked to Mr. Hawkins that on such a night a lookout was of little use, as before a vessel or any other object could be seen, the ship's way could not be stopped or changed in time to avert the danger.

"It is a risk we have got to run," said Mr. Hawkins. "If any small coasting vessel, or fishing craft bound to George's Bank, should be in our path, the Lord have mercy on the poor fellows on board."

"Amen!" said Mr. Digges, with an irreverent laugh. "But the Rosamond has staunch bows, and my motto is, 'Let the hardest fend off!'" He then stepped forward into the waist, and addressing the group of sailors standing by the windlass, told them to keep their peepers peeled, and keep a sharp lookout.

The order was hardly given, when Jack Radkin, who was standing by the bowsprit bitts, called out, "Port your helm! hard-a-port! a sail right ahead!"

179

And a black mass, blacker than the almost Cimmerian darkness around, could be discerned about a point on the larboard bow. It proved to be a small schooner, on a wind, steering to the eastward, and crossing the bow of the ship.

While Mr. Digges rushed forward to the bows to see more clearly the character of the danger, Captain Lamark reiterated the directions given by Jack Radkin, and Mr. Hawkins sprung to the wheel, and with a vigorous arm forced the tiller hard-a-port.

It was too late! The ship struck the schooner nearly amidships, and crushed, capsized, and demolished the little vessel, so that no remnant of her or her crew was ever afterwards seen, and hardly recoiling from or staggering on account of the destructive blow she had given, passed onward on her way, amid the terrific screams and agonizing cries of the unfortunate men, thus called upon in the dead of night, without a note of warning, to appear before their Creator and answer for their sins !

The Rosamond was hove-to as soon as it was practicable, with a view to render assistance to the drowning sailors, and ascertain the amount of injury the ship had sustained in the conflict. But it was found impossible, on that dark and stormy night, to rescue any of the sinking men from their dreadful fate, or even to find the spot where the collision took place. On examining the bows of the ship, it was ascertained that the cutwater was carried away; also the martingale; the jib-boom was broken short off, probably by coming in contact with one of the schooner's masts. The bowsprit was a little shaky, which endangered the stability of the foremast, but the ship had sprung no leak, and in half an hour was in a condition to proceed on her route.

But where was Mr. Digges? In the confusion incident to the shock, this officer for some time was not missed. But when summoned by the captain to receive some instructions, he could not be found. He was not in the ship! When last seen he was standing between the knight-heads, just as the vessels came in contact, and in all likelihood was knocked overboard by the shock, or by one of the falling spars.

And thus Mark Rowland, before he reached his home, witnessed another thrilling scene, illustrating the danger which attends a sailor's occupation, and the uncertainty of life among "those who go down to the sea in ships, and do business on the great waters."

Soon after sunrise the next morning, the wind hauled round to the south-west, and soon afterwards died away. The clouds and mists dispersed, and the blessed sun shone forth as if to gladden the hearts of the ship's company, after the dark scenes they had passed through. Mark was early aloft, and gazing intently on the western horizon, in expectation of seeing the land or a light-house, but no such welcome object met his view. As he cast his eyes over the waters, he beheld a number of vessels of different characters, and evidently bound in different directions. Sloops, schooners, brigs, and ships, fishing-smacks, coasters, yachts, European traders, and Indiamen, showing beyond all doubt that the Rosamond was approaching a wealthy seaport, or a coast rich in the commerce and enterprise of the inhabitants.

While he was admiring the scene, his heart overflowing with joy at this evidence of the near termination of his maritime adventures, his attention was arrested by the spouting of a couple of whales, not a hundred fathoms off, crossing the bows. They soon afterwards showed themselves under the stern, came up on the quarter, spouted, and disappeared in the depths of the ocean, thrusting up their tails and splashing the water about at a great rate as they went down.

They soon made their appearance again, and began to frolic around the ship, and continued their antics until Mr. Hawkins became offended at the liberties they were taking,

16

and expressed a fear that unless rebuked they might become too familiar, and ordered the steward to hand him a fowling-piece from the cabin. This he loaded with a ball, and the next time the huge, uncouth-looking monsters came up to spout, he took deliberate aim at the back of the nearest one, and fired.   .

That the bullet struck the whale there was no doubt, and such an unkind salutation evidently made upon their minds an unfavorable impression of our hospitality, for they sank beneath the waters, sheered off, and sought some other field for the practice of their gymnastic exercises. .

Among those who closely watched these proceedings was Archie Stobbs.   Notwithstanding he enacted the part of Amphitrite when crossing the line, there was little in the appearance of Archie that bordered on the feminine, excepting his diminutive proportions.   His features exhibited a ludicrous absence of symmetry, were weather-beaten and case-hardened, having been a countless number of times soaked in salt water and dried in the tropical sun.   He had voyaged to almost every part of the world, and had met with many curious adventures.   He took a deep interest in this visit from these oily strangers, and exhibited anxiety and displeasure when Mr. Hawkins proceeded to compliment them with a bullet.

· Mark took notice of the change in Archie's manner, habitually gay and cheerful, as the whales began to spout, and listened with surprise to his murmur of satisfaction, when it became evident that these clumsy monsters had gone off on a cruise.   Seeing Archie looking over the bow in the direction which the strangers had apparently taken, Mark approached him, and inquired if he knew anything about whales?

"About whales?" replied Archie ; "to be sure I do. I once shipped on a whaling-voyage, and passed through scenes of a rough-and-tumble character which I shall never forget, if I live to be a hundred years old. My flesh always creeps when I see a whale, and I am willing that he should pass on his way without being checked or annoyed."

"Archie," said Mark, with a persuasive smile, "I wish you would tell me something about those rough-and-tumble scenes you speak of. The whale is an interesting animal, but I know little of his character or habits. That there are many perils in the whale-fishery I have often heard."

"Perils enough, my lad," said Archie, "to satisfy any reasonable person. They won't catch me in a whaling-ship again, anyhow. If you want to know something of my experience in the business of whale-catching, I will give it to you with pleasure."

Mark assured the good-natured tar that nothing would give him greater satisfaction, upon which Archie turned round, hitched up his trowsers, put his finger on his temple in a reflective mood, then seated himself on the bowsprit bitts, and shot ahead in the following style:

"My young friend, I once found myself in Rio Janeiro, without money, friends, or a ship, which I hope will never prove to be your case, when the whaling barque Loon, belonging to Nantucket, put into the harbor for supplies. The barque was in want of men, having lost a whole boat's-crew in an encounter with a sperm whale about a week before she arrived in port. I gladly seized the opportunity to join her and embark on a whaling-voyage. On leaving Rio we steered directly for the Brazil Banks, a famous place for whales, and men were stationed at the mast-head all day long on the lookout.

"One morning a cry was heard from aloft: 'There she spouts! There she spouts! An eighty-barrel whale, as sure as I'm a sinner!'

"'Where away?' shouted Captain Stockman.

"'Under the lee beam, about a couple of miles off!' was
the reply.

"The bark was put off before the wind, the yards were
squared, and we ran down towards the big fish. All was
excitement. Our three whale-boats were ready for action,
and every man seemed eager to make the attack. I was
stationed in the second mate's boat, and as we neared the
fish the bark was hove-to, and the word was given to lower
away the boats and shove off. And away we went in full
chase after the whale.

"And now ensued a trial of strength and skill of a most
exciting character. The boats were commanded by the captain and the two mates, each of whom seemed madly bent
on reaching the whale first, and sending a harpoon into his
body.

"I must confess I did not share the enthusiasm of the
officers and those of the crew who had been long in the
business. A whale is a powerful fish, and when in his tan-
trums difficult to manage. The stories I had heard about
him did not place his character in the most amiable light.
I felt somewhat nervous as we drew towards the monster,
and would have given all my profits on the voyage to have
exchanged places with the ship-keeper who was left on board.
But it could not be. I was fairly in for it, and pulled heartily
at my oar, and tried to wear a bold face.

"I soon heard the captain and chief mate earnestly encouraging the men in their respective boats to exert all their
strength to win the race, and Mr. Kamworth, the second
mate, who steered our boat, a tall and powerful man, was
not behind-hand in urging the men to the work.

"'Pull men!' said he. 'Do pull! Bend your backs to
the oars! Send her ahead, like good fellows! Let's be first
alongside! Do pull for once in your lives! Mr. Garvill's
boat is gaining on us! Why don't you pull, you miserable,

lazy ragamuffins? Why don't you lay out your strength? That's right! There she shoots ahead! Hurrah, keep that stroke, and we shall be first on his hump! Stand by, harpooner! Stand by, and give it to him good!'

"When the whale rose again to the surface to spout, our boat was about an oar's length ahead of the captain's boat, and Mr. Kamworth steered directly for the body of the whale. As the boat came in contact with the fish, the harpooner, standing in the bow of the boat, threw his instrument with all the force of which he was master into the back of the huge animal, at the same time exclaiming, 'Stern all!' which was an order to back the boat astern with all possible dispatch, in order to avoid a blow from the big fish's tail while he was going down.

"And down he went — down—down, carrying with him an immense length of line which was attached to the harpoon. A hundred fathoms at least ran out before the line began to slacken, a sign that he was again coming to the surface to spout or breathe. We hauled upon the line to keep it tight, while the persecuted animal rose to the top of the water, when Mr. Kamworth was ready to thrust the deadly lance into his vitals. The other boats were also on hand, and their commanders with their lances assisted in the work.

"The whale again, convulsed with agony, disappeared from view, but soon rose, and a shout of exultation sounded over the water, from the crews of the boats, as they beheld the monster *spouting blood!* a sign that he had received his mortal wound. He lashed the waves with his enormous tail, and made tremendous struggles in his dying moments, but luckily the boats were kept out of his reach. His struggles were too violent to last long. He turned over on his side, and floated, a lifeless mass.

" The boats were fastened to the carcass, which was soon towed alongside the ship. Tackles were made fast to it to keep it steady, and the operation of "flenching" commenced; that is, stripping the blubber from the back and sides, and stowing it away on board, where it was afterwards tried out in immense try-pots. Being thus converted into oil, it was deposited in casks, that were stowed in the hold.

"A few days after this successful attack on the whale, and the whole operation was a new and deeply interesting one to me, we made war upon another of these ponderous creatures. This proved to be a sperm whale, and an ugly, obstinate fellow into the bargain. He was struck by the captain, and went down as if changed into lead. When he came up, either by accident or design, he rose directly beneath the second mate's boat, in which I was stationed, which he struck with such force as to send it flying a dozen feet in the air and spilling out the men and other contents, in the most awkward and extraordinary manner imaginable. The boat was shattered to pieces, and I was landed on the back of the whale, stupified and badly hurt by the fall, and hardly knowing what course to take.

"'Jump overboard!' exclaimed the captain, who was in his boat a few fathoms off, calmly surveying the scene, 'and we will pick you up.'

"The whale, however, saved me the trouble; for before I could collect my scattered senses, he turned a sort of half somerset, and threw me from his back into the water. As my arm was broken in the fracas, and I never was much of a swimmer, I should have been drowned had not the other boats been at hand. Mr. Kamworth and one other of the boat's crew were never seen after the boat was demolished. The others were all saved without having received any serious injury. Not having a chance to send a lance into this whale, the rascal got away, carrying with him a couple of harpoons, which must have tickled him to some purpose, and two tubs of whale line.

"Several weeks passed before I was able to attend to my duties, for, besides my broken arm, a couple of my ribs were fractured, and what was of more importance, my nose was put out of joint by a blow from one of the boat's thwarts, and my beauty was spoiled forever! While I was laid up, the ship's company had managed to capture another of these big fish, but the captain, disgusted with such slow work, determined to change his fishing-ground, and accordingly we passed around Cape Horn, and entered the Pacific Ocean.

"This proved to be a most unfortunate movement for the owner, captain, and all hands. For my own part, I had already got enough of the whaling business to satisfy any reasonable man, and should have been well content to have gone home with half a cargo of oil; but I was destined to see more of the pleasant mysteries of the whale-fishery; enough to last me my lifetime, should I live as many years as Methuselah.

"One day, while cruising for sperm whales, we fell in with a monster of a fish. Captain Stockman, who had followed the business for many years, said it was the largest whale he ever met with, being at least one hundred feet in length. He was an old cruiser, full of wickedness, a stranger to fear, and probably owed the whalemen a grudge. It required courage to attack a sperm whale of that size and character, for they are exceedingly knowing, and sometimes exercise their immense strength and power in a way which completely turns the tables on their antagonists. Captain Stockman, however, declared that he feared no whale that ever spouted, and ordered the boats to be lowered. Away we went, full of life and energy, with a determination to attack and conquer this king of whales.

" The captain took the lead in the chase, but he was closely followed by the other boats. The whale was moving lazily about on the top of the water as the boat approached him, and the harpooner thrust two irons, one after the other, into his massive sides. This unprovoked attack awakened him with a vengeance. But instead of going down, in order to escape from his enemies, and showing us his flukes, as a decent and well-behaved whale would have done, he turned short round on his heel to face them and fight them.

" He saw the captain's boat, which was not ten fathoms off, and rushed towards it with his jaws wide open. And, my lad, you cannot conceive of a more dreadful, appalling sight, than was witnessed by that ship's company, as the angry monster rushed upon the boat.

" ' Pull for your lives, men! ' screamed the captain. But the men were stupified with horror. They uttered in chorus one agonizing shriek, and the whale was upon them. He seized the boat between his enormous jaws, and crushed it like a craw-fish. The boat's crew, with one exception, barely saved themselves from instant death by leaping into the water. Poor Bob Merlin, whom fear had robbed of his strength, shared the fate of the boat. The captain and the remainder of the boat's crew were picked up by the two other boats.

" Our attention was directed to the strange conduct of the whale. He seemed really mad, swimming about on the surface, and furiously lashing the water with his tail. After amusing himself in this manner a few minutes, he steered a course which led him nearer the barque, which was still lying-to. He soon saw the barque, and regarded her as his mortal foe on which he was determined to wreak his vengeance, for he increased his speed, and altered his course, steering directly for the vessel.

" The savage animal rushed towards her with his mouth

open, to the great terror of our shipkeeper and cook, the only persons on board. He seized the ship by the bends with his teeth, and vainly attempted to demolish what he undoubtedly supposed to be a huge animal. But finding his efforts unsuccessful, as if gifted with reason, he went another way to work. He turned round and swam off some thirty or forty fathoms, then again changed front, and rushed with almost lightning speed, directly towards the ship.

" His mouth was not open this time, but his hard, bony, and enormous· head struck the barque Loon on the starboard bow, just beneath the fore chain-wales, with all the force of a gigantic battering-ram, and crushed in the planks and timbers, making a wide hole, through which the water rushed like a sluice-way. The ship filled in a few minutes and fell over on her beam-ends.

" The mad whale, as if satisfied with the vengeance he had inflicted on his enemies, turned about, and passing between the two boats, which he did not seem to notice, and with the two harpoons, whale lines and all, still sticking in his side, swam rapidly off to the southward, and was soon lost to view.

" We were now in a most distressing condition. Twenty men in two whale-boats, adrift on the broad Pacific, without sails, provisions, or water, excepting a couple of kegs which had been put in the boats for immediate use, when the boats first left the barque. The barque was full of water, and the waves were breaking· over her sides and decks, so we could get nothing from the hold or steerage. Lingering death by starvation seemed to be our certain destiny. In that hour of distress, Captain Stockman, who was a pious man, prayed to our heavenly Father to assist us and save us.

" The men were equally divided between the two boats. The captain took charge of one and the chief mate the other. According to the captain's reckoning we were nearly in the latitude of the island of Masafuera when the disaster took place, and about two hundred miles to the westward. This island was the nearest land, and the captain ordered the oars to be manned, and the boats to be pulled in that direction, the course being indicated by the compass, there being one in each boat, by day, and by the moon and. stars by night.

" The captain encouraged us all by his example and his cheering words. ·He recommended that one half of. each boat's crew should labor at the oars while the others took their rest. And he assured us that if we worked hard and constantly, we might, with divine assistance, reach the land before we became entirely exhausted by want of sustenance.

" There was comfort in his words, for life is sweet, and a man will do much to prolong his days, however miserable they may be. We promised to act on his suggestion, and obey him in everything; and just as night came on, we started off for the island of Masafuera, with the sea tolerably smooth, and the wind light from the southward. And a hard time we had of it, Mark, I assure you ; but we kept the boat going through the water with her bows pointed towards the island. We encouraged each other as well as we could, and· bore our deprivations manfully, and during the first twenty-four hours we must have proceeded at least a hundred miles.

" The boats kept company through the first night and the following day, but on the second night the men became weary, and suffered much for want of food and water, the small quantity which we had in the boats when we left the ship affording but slight relief. Their efforts at the oars were not so steady and uninterrupted as at first. In the middle of the night a squall arose, and we lost sight of our companion, I being in the captain's boat, and we had much ado to keep the boat head to wind, to prevent her being swamped.

"Towards morning the wind died away, and the sea became comparatively smooth, and before the sun rose we looked around with much anxiety for our consort, but to our great grief and disappointment no boat was to be seen. The sea had undoubtedly swept over her during the height of the squall, and my unfortunate shipmates were drowned.

"On the third evening of our perilous voyage, soon after sunset, having been about forty-eight hours in the boat, deprived of all sustenance, and almost dying of fatigue and hunger, the captain, whose courage and hope never for a moment deserted him, after gazing intently in the direction which we were steering, with a joyful shout announced the glad tidings that *land was in sight!* and directed our attention to what appeared to be a low, dark, ragged cloud, resting on the eastern horizon. This he told us was the island of Masafuera.

"We moved slowly through the water the following night, after resting on our oars, lest we should pass the island in the darkness; and when morning came, the island, a mass of barren rocks, rising more than two thousand feet above sea, was not more than fifteen miles off. With a good will we pulled towards it, selected a spot where we could land in safety, and sprang upon the shore, grateful to God for his signal mercy in saving us from destruction.

"But our situation even now was far from enviable. Masafuera is an uninhabited island about ten miles in circumference, possessing no vegetation, and providing but scant means for sustaining life. And our spirits were by no means cheered by finding not far from the spot on which we landed, and only a few fathoms from the beach, two human skeletons, which told us a fearful story of suffering, and lingering death by starvation.

"We found some water in the hollows of rocks, which greatly refreshed us; we also procured some shell-fish, and knocked over a few birds, which we ate with a good appetite without cooking. But if we had had no boat by which to leave the island, we should have been worse off than you were on the island of St. Paul, with a far more distant prospect of being taken off by some passing vessel.

"After tarrying on the island a couple of days, and recovering somewhat from our fatigue, we again embarked in our boat, still steering to the eastward, and on the second day in the afternoon happily succeeded in landing on the famous island of Juan Fernandez, where Robinson Crusoe many years ago experienced some strange adventures, which I dare say you have read about, Mark. We found on the island some hospitable people, who treated us with kindness, and provided us with the means of reaching Valparaiso. From that port I worked my passage in a ship to Boston, and of one thing I am certain, you will never catch me in a whaling ship again. And as for whales, I always like to give them a good berth, with the full understanding that if they will let me alone, I will let them alone."

CHAPTER XVI.

IT was about eight o'clock when the breeze sprung up from the southward, and in an hour afterwards, bearing three points on the weather-bow, and looming up from the haze which still hung low, Mark Rowland saw from aloft the whole structure of the lofty light-house, and the high, uneven lands on the back of Cape Cod.

"Land ho!" he shouted, with delight, and hastened down on deck.

"Land ho!" was joyfully responded by the officers and men. "Hurrah! Cape Cod is in sight!"

The land could now be seen from the deck, and the course of the ship being slightly altered, and the sails trimmed accordingly, she rapidly approached that wild-looking, uninviting coast, the first land seen by the Pilgrim Fathers, which in the gloomy month of December must have looked terribly grim and forbidding; and by twelve o'clock that day the ship was up with Race Point, and had fairly entered Massachusetts Bay.

The harbor of Provincetown was now plainly in sight, and soon was seen the range of coast in the vicinity of Plymouth, immortalized by the landing of the Pilgrim Fathers, and, in swift succession, the high lands of Marshfield, Cohasset Rocks, the Blue Hills in the distance, Boston light-house, and Point Alderton, with the dark and broken ledges of rocks which line the entrance to Boston harbor, while ships, brigs, schooners, sloops, and sail-boats, with their snow-white sails, dotted the smooth sea in every direction.

As Mark Rowland gazed admiringly on the scene, and spoke enthusiastically in its praise, old Jack Radkin shook his head, and showed by his looks that the scene had no charms for him.

" Is not this a cheerful sight, Jack?" inquired Mark. " Can there be anything more beautiful than Massachusetts Bay? How mild and balmy the atmosphere! How smooth the waters! How clear and distinct the wavy outline of the land!"

" Oh," replied Jack, with a grim smile, "this is all well enough at this pleasant season of the year, returning home in a fine ship, with a quiet sea and a fair wind. But to judge fairly of its character, you should see it in a heavy north-east gale, *blowing right on shore*, with a raging sea like a range of young mountains, rolling in all the way from Cape Sable; the weather thick and rainy; breakers ahead or under your lee on either tack; your ship deeply laden, and driven almost bodily to leeward; and you have the choice of two evils, — to cut away your masts by the deck, let go all your anchors, and try to ride it out in poor holding ground, or plump her ashore on the beach, with about one chance in ten of reaching the shore alive."

" If you want to see Boston Bay in all its glory," said Archie Stobbs, joining in the conversation, " you should come on the coast, as I have done, in the winter season, in a leaky ship, after a long passage across the Atlantic, short of provisions and water, sails all blown to pieces, men worn out and discouraged with hard work, famine, and exposure; your ship covered with a solid body of ice a foot thick; running rigging too-stiff to be used; the thick sheets of spray dashing over the decks, fore and aft; the forecastle, bed-clothes, and jackets, soaked with salt water, and the wind blowing 'a hurricane *directly out of the bay*, with the thermometer at zero! Ah, my lad, if you were to witness a few scenes of this description, you would know how to value plenty of sea-room, off soundings, and talk less about a sailor's pleasures in coming on the coast."

"I talk of it as I find it," said Mark; "but, after this description of your experience, Archie, and Jack Radkin's glowing account of the charms of Massachusetts Bay in a north-east storm, you will never catch *me* coming on the New-England coast in the winter season;" and he added, in a lower tone, "*or in any other season.*"

If the truth must be told, Mark's adventures on the island of St. Paul, and the dark scenes he had witnessed, typical of a sailor's life, had no attractions in his eyes; they were by no means to his taste. Indeed, he was strongly inclined to believe that those who wrote prose and poetry in praise of the sea, and described in glowing terms the pleasurable excitement, the wild joys and sunshine of a sailor's life, were little better than arrant humbugs, and either knew nothing of the trials, temptations, and perils, of a life at sea, or, like the fox who had lost his tail, were desirous that others should undergo the same pain and humiliation which he himself had suffered.

His bosom throbbed with delight at the near prospect of embracing his mother and the dear ones whom he left in the humble cottage at Glenmaple. But his features became clouded with apprehension, when he reflected that a year and a half had passed since he left his home, and unforeseen evils might have befallen them during his absence. He determined, however, that, if he should succeed in getting once more snugly seated at his mother's fireside, he would never voluntarily separate from her again; their fortunes, whether for weal or woe, henceforth should be the same.

The ship Rosamond arrived off Boston light-house about six o'clock in the evening, but the wind being light, and the tide on the ebb, it was found expedient to anchor in the roads, and the ship did not reach the city until the next morning.

It was about ten o'clock when Mark lightly bounded on the wharf, and, with a joyous heart, proceeded to the counting-room of Mr. Fortesque. That gentleman did not immediately recognize him, rigged as he was in a neat and becoming suit of clothes, purchased at the Cape of Good Hope, and rejoicing in features bronzed by exposure to the sun for many months; besides, Mark had grown nearly a head taller, and looked far more like a man than the simple country lad whom he parted with on the wharf some eighteen months before.

But when Mr. Fortesque found it was Mark Rowland who was before him, the bright-looking boy who had left Boston in the ship Saladin, and whom he believed to have been lost by some mishap on the island of St. Paul, he eagerly grasped his hand, and could hardly contain his astonishment and pleasure. He made him sit down, and give a full description of his adventures, to which he listened with intense interest. When Mark had finished his story, Mr. Fortesque again shook him by the hand, congratulated him on his good fortune in escaping from the island and taking with him such a rich prize, and promised to be a friend to him through life. He advised him in regard to the disposition of the merchandise belonging to him on board the Rosamond, and supplied him with money for his immediate wants, and thus anticipated the kind offers of the generous-hearted Captain Lamark.

The next morning Mark Rowland, with buoyant spirits, 'entered the railroad car which would convey him some thirty miles on the route towards his native village of Glenmaple.

The mode of conveyance was new to him, but he liked it on account of the rapidity with which it hurried him towards his home. Soon after he was seated, a gentleman with his wife and a little girl came into the car. The lady and gentleman took the seat immediately behind him; while the girl, a bright-eyed, intelligent-looking fairy, some ten or twelve years of age, took the vacant seat by his side. The cars started, and Mark and the little girl engaged in conversation, which to him was a source of great pleasure, as he had so long been debarred from the society of those sweeteners of existence, — women and children.

The attention of Mark was soon arrested by a name which was marked on the kerchief which the girl held in her hand, " *Ella Rivington!*"

" Is that *your* name? " said he.

" Yes," she replied.

" What is your father's name?"

" James Stanley Rivington."

," Where is your father *now?* " inquired Mark, in a voice and manner so excited as almost to frighten the little girl.

" There he sits, right behind you," said she.

Mark turned his head quickly, and found himself face to face with Mr. and Mrs. Rivington, the same persons who were rescued from the wreck of the ship Clarion, of Salem, on the passage of the ship Saladin towards the equator.

Mr. Rivington had but recently arrived from South America. He was still connected with a mercantile house in Boston, doing a large business with Brazil, and, with his wife and daughter, was now on a visit to his parents, who resided in a town forty miles from Boston, and through which the railroad passed.

One of the first acts of Mr. Rivington on his arrival at Boston, was to call on Mr. Fortesque, the owner of the ship Saladin, and express his deep sense of the noble conduct of

17*

Captain Somers and the whole ship's company, in rescuing him and his wife from a dreadful death, and ministering to their comfort after they were taken on board the ship. He spoke in exalted terms of the activity, intelligence, and worth of the cabin-boy, Mark Rowland, in whose success in life he said he felt an especial interest, and was greatly shocked to learn he had met with a fatal accident on a desert isle in the midst of the ocean.

This unexpected rencounter in a railroad car was, indeed, a joyous one. Mr. Rivington owed Mark a debt of gratitude for having discovered the sunken wreck, and he and his wife had deeply mourned what they believed to be his sad and untimely fate. They indulged in heartfelt pleasure at meeting him again; at not only finding him alive, but improved in strength, beauty, and manliness.

The sailor-boy and the merchant had much to say to each other, and it seemed as if they had hardly exchanged congratulations, before the train reached the station at which Mark was to take the stage-coach to Glenmaple. Anxious to see his mother, Mark resisted the pressing invitation of Mr. and Mrs. Rivington to go on with them, and pass a day or two with their relations.

" Well, Mark," said Mr. Rivington, "I shall be absent from my business but a few days, and when you return to Boston, I shall expect you to come directly to my house. It is easily found, and you may be sure of a hearty welcome."

" Yes," added Mrs. Rivington, "you must take up your abode with us while you are in the city. I shall always look upon you as a near and valued friend, — as belonging to us."

Mark was greatly embarrassed by such manifestations of kindness, and was proceeding to disclaim any merit or services on his part that entitled him to such favor, when he was interrupted by little Ella, who said, "Oh, you *must*

come, Mark. You don't know how much father and mother
have talked about you since they came home; and mother
cried when she told me how you fell off the rocks into the
sea, and was drowned. Promise me that you will come."

Mark Rowland promised.

He had to wait fully an hour at the railway station, before
the stage was ready to start; and that hour, while he was
lounging about the rooms, jostling against strangers in
whom he took no interest, and watching the movements
of the clock, which he thought, once or twice, had stopped,
it moved so slow, seemed the longest hour of his life.

But time passed onward with steady, measured steps, and
the stage-coach made its appearance. The driver promised
Mark that before sunset he should be safely landed within
a stone's throw of his mother's door. The roads were in
good condition, and the horses travelled rapidly over the
ground, but to Mark they seemed to be crawling along at a
snail's pace.

Notwithstanding his impatience to get to the end of his
journey, when he reached the farm-house in Westville, where
he was so hospitably entertained on his journey to Boston, he
called on the driver to stop. He recognized the place, and
saw Mr. Drummond, with his well-remembered, benevolent
visage, near the doorway, busy about some ",chores." Mark
jumped out of the coach, and grasped the astonished farmer
by the hand, who could hardly be persuaded that this was
the boy who had once passed a night beneath his roof, on
his way to the great city, determined to try his fortunes on
the sea.

Mr. Drummond called out his wife, who greeted Mark
right cordially; for the kind-hearted couple had felt quite an
interest in his success, and had often talked of him during
the past year, and wondered what had been the result of his
boyish enterprise.

After a few minutes conversation, at a hint from the driver, Mark resumed his seat. The stage-coach passed on. And while Mark is on his way to visit his dearly-loved home, we will take a look at some other persons, and inquire into events which occurred at Glenmaple, while he was a solitary inhabitant of the island of St. Paul, or witnessing the strange scenes which chequer the life of a sailor.

CHAPTER XVII.

THE ship Saladin, in which Mark Rowland sailed from Boston, after having encountered the furious squall near the island of St. Paul, and being driven away to leeward, proceeded slowly on her way, attempting to get to the southward, Captain Somers deeply lamenting the fatal accident that had befallen the cabin-boy, who was, as has already been remarked, a general favorite. The captain, after hearing the representations of Mr. Smeaton, the second mate, did not for a moment doubt that the little fellow had fallen from a precipice into the deep water at its base, and, notwithstanding his skill as a swimmer, had been drowned. Even if he had reason to suppose Mark might still be alive on that barren island, any attempt to render him assistance would have been unsuccessful, as the deeply-laden ship, after running off so far to leeward, could never have beat up to the island against the trade-wind and a strong current. Captain Somers shuddered when he thought of the fate of the poor boy who was intrusted to his charge by Mr. Fortesque, and who promised to prove himself worthy of the interest which that merchant took in his fortunes. He shuddered when he thought of the anguish his friends would experience when they should hear of his melancholy fate.

I have already said that the Saladin was a dull-sailing ship, and after putting Mr. and Mrs. Rivington on board a vessel bound to Pernambuco, this vessel continued to fall to leeward of her route, insomuch that Captain Somers deemed it expedient to put into some port in Brazil, in order to procure a supply of provisions. Accordingly, in three weeks after leaving the island of St. Paul, the ship entered the port of San Salvador, or as it is often called, Bahia, situated on the north-western side of the large and beautiful Bay of All Saints. From this port Captain Somers wrote to his employer, Mr. Fortesque, and gave him all the particulars relating to the landing of the boat's crew on the island of St. Paul, and the supposed melancholy fate of Mark Rowland. Mr. Fortesque was grieved at the intelligence; he had taken a great fancy to Mark, and predicted that he would make his way successfully through the world. He lost no time in writing a letter to Mrs. Rowland, acquainting her with the sad event, condoling with her on her irreparable misfortune, and giving her words of consolation and kindness.

But how shall I describe the anguish of the afflicted widow when she read the letter which conveyed intelligence of the death of her son. "He had fallen from a high cliff" — so ran the words — "into the sea beneath, and was drowned."

After reading this sad missive, the language of which was terribly explicit, Mrs. Rowland could not cherish the slightest hope of ever seeing her son again. "My brave boy!" she exclaimed. "He exposed himself to the perils which beset the life of a sailor, not altogether because he longed for a roving life, and yearned to see more of the world and mingle in its busiest scenes, but chiefly for the purpose of contributing to my support, and that of his brother and sister. He went abroad to diminish my cares, and furnish us all with the necessaries and comforts of life. My noble boy! To meet such a terrible death far away from his home! I shall never see him again on earth, but we shall meet in heaven."

The fate of Mark Rowland was soon known in the village of Glenmaple, and many friendly persons called upon the widow to console her in affliction, and whisper words of comfort in her ear. But their well-meant kindness failed to produce the effect intended. She felt grateful for the sympathy of her neighbors, but she was crushed to the earth by the weight of her sorrow.

More than twelve months passed away after she heard of the death of her son, and Time, " the great consoler," had brought no sunshine to her heart. Her features, pallid and wan, were overspread with a settled gloom. Her thoughts still dwelt unceasingly on the excellence and affection of her boy. Tokens of his devoted love, his industry, and his wisdom above his years, met her at every turn, and re-awakened from hour to hour her deep-seated grief.

Nevertheless, the heart-stricken widow did not forget that two lovely and promising children still clung to her for support. Since she learned that Mark had perished, she loved them, if possible, with a more devoted affection than before. Instead of remitting her usual labors, and abandoning herself to grief, she worked harder than ever, insomuch that her health, never robust, gave way, and she saw before her but a dark and gloomy prospect, in the foreground of which stood Poverty and Disease, and, in the background, the Almshouse and a tomb!

Mrs. Rowland was one afternoon seated at the back window of her little cottage. She was feeble, and unusually pale, for she had that day exerted herself beyond her strength. The hand of sorrow and sickness had drawn deep furrows across her once radiant and becoming features. She had sent her little boy, Albert, on an errand to procure a loaf of bread, for neither herself nor children had tasted aught since their scanty morning meal, and she had no resources for the following day. Little Ellen was seated on a cricket by her side, reading aloud some passages from a story-book that had been given her by one of her school-mates.

Mrs. Rowland appeared to be listening attentively, but her mind was elsewhere. She was thinking of her poverty, of her broken health, and the destitute condition to which her children would be reduced, if she, their only stay and sup-port, should be removed by the hand of death. The sun was sinking beneath a distant range of hills in the west, which, perhaps, added to the depression of her spirits.

At this moment Albert rushed into the house, his face flushed with excitement, and exclaimed, with an animated voice, " Oh, mother, the stage has just stopped at the head of the lane, and a strange gentleman has got out, with a big trunk; and he is coming towards the house ! "

It was so seldom that a case of this kind occurred, — for the poor and humble have few visitors, — that Mrs. Rowland was startled at the abrupt announcement. " Who is it, Albert ? " inquired the widow of her son.

" I don't know," said Albert ; " but I guess he does not mean any harm, mother, for he looks as smiling and happy as if he had good news to tell you."

A sort of indefinite sensation, akin to hope, passed through the bosom of the widow at this intelligence ; but tarried only for an instant. She felt there was no room for hope. She rose from her chair, and, with steps unsteady through weakness, walked towards the door to inquire the business of the stranger, who, with features lighted up with smiles, was about to visit the abode of sorrow, want, and disease.

She heard a step on the threshold. She lifted the latch, and beheld before her, with eyes sparkling with rapture, and a ruddy, sun-burnt visage, expressing the best emotions of the human heart, her long-lost boy, her son Mark, whose death she had for many months unceasingly mourned.

"Mother!" exclaimed Mark, in a well-remembered voice, "dear mother! I have come back to bring you joy and competence; and we shall never part again."

Mrs. Rowland was so overcome by her feelings, so overwhelmed with joy and astonishment combined, that it was some minutes before she was able to say a word. She wept, and kissed her long-lost son in silence; and, prompted by a feeling of piety, of gratitude towards her Maker for restoring the lost one to her arms, sunk on her knees, and poured out her fervent thanks for the blessing with which she was crowned.

It is hardly necessary to say that, after the entrance of Mark, there was no longer hunger or sorrow in that humble dwelling. Provisions in abundance were procured from the nearest inn, and the children, as well as the mother, made a joyous meal. And I question whether kings or princes, in their gorgeous palaces, ever tasted a delight more pure and exstatic than was enjoyed by that humble and virtuous family that evening, while the sailor-boy was relating the tale of his adventures, and ever and anon answering the never-ending questions of his brother and sister.

Mrs. Rowland clung closely to her son, as if she feared the whole was a blissful dream, and that she might in a few minutes awake to find her joy changed to sorrow, and the cottage again turned into a place of mourning. It was at a late hour when the members of that now happy family retired to rest.

My tale is finished. Mr. Fortesque, as well as Mr. Rivington and Captain Lamark, proved a faithful friend to Mark Rowland. The treasure which the forlorn sailor-boy found among the rocks on the island of St. Paul was increased by the prudent management of Captain Lamark, and

18

being judiciously invested, produced a handsome annual income. Mark was thus enabled to gratify the darling wish of his heart, — improve his education ; and also extend that blessing, with many others, to his brother Albert and his sister Ellen.

His eighteen months' cruise in the ships Saladin and Rosamond, including his sufferings for months on a desert island, banished from the mind of Mark Rowland any yearnings after wild adventures and salt-water scenes. At a proper time he entered the counting-room of Rivington & Co., in Boston; and applied himself unremittingly to his duties, being determined to qualify himself to become, not " a merchant prince," or any other kind of prince, but a Boston Merchant, in the truest and noblest sense of the term. His happiness was established on a firm basis, when he secured the affections of Ella Rivington, a bright and blooming woman, every way fitted to be the companion and wife of a man of intelligence and worth.

They were married; and Mark became a partner in the firm. He is now at its head, and is known as a highly respected, useful, and influential member of society. He is philosopher enough to enjoy, in their fullest extent, and with feelings of pious gratitude, the blessings with which he is crowned, and Christian enough to thank God that he is *able* as well as *willing* to minister to the happiness of others.

THE END.

MARGARET AND HER BRIDESMAIDS,

By the Author of "THE QUEEN OF THE COUNTY."

1 vol., 12mo.   Elegant fancy cloth.   Price $1.75.

This fascinating story of "Six School Girls" is as charming a story as has been written for young ladies.   The
talented author has a great reputation in England, and all
her books are widely circulated and read.   "Faith Gartney's
Girlhood" and "Margaret and her Bridesmaids" should
stand side by side in every young lady's book-case.   Read
what the *London Athenæum*, the highest literary authority,
says of it: "We may save ourselves the trouble of giving
any lengthened review of this book, for we recommend all
who are in search of a fascinating novel to read it for themselves.   They will find it well worth their while.   There is a
freshness and originality about it quite charming, and there
is a certain nobleness in the treatment, both of sentiment
and incident, which is not often found.   We imagine that
few can read it without deriving some comfort or profit from
the quiet good sense and unobtrusive words of counsel with
which it abounds."

The story is very interesting.   It is the history of six
school-fellows.   Margaret, the heroine, is, of course, a
woman in the highest state of perfection.   But Lotty — the
little, wilful, wild, fascinating, brave Lotty — is the gem of
the book, and, as far as our experience in novel reading goes,
is an entirely original character — a creation — and a very
charming one.   No story that occurs to our memory contains
more interest than this for novel readers, particularly those
of the tender sex, to whom it will be a dear favorite.

We hope the authoress will give us some more novels, as
good as "Margaret and her Bridesmaids."

THE QUEEN OF THE COUNTY,

By the Author of "MARGARET AND HER BRIDESMAIDS."

1 vol., 12mo.   Elegant fancy cloth.   Price $1.75.

Of all the books published or republished by Mr. Loring, this
winter, this is the best. Yet when asked what we like so much in
it, we find it difficult to tell and leave our explanations midway, to
indulge in such young-ladyisms as "Charming!" "Delightful!"
"Beautiful!" Is the story new? Oh, no, it is quite common, a
mere love story, a fall from a horse, a declaration of love, a death
or two. Has it character? Again, no. The persons written about
are every day characters. We come then to the style of the book,—
what of that? Ah, yes, now we have it,—herein lies the charm;
not the diction merely, but in the simple unassuming way in which
the story is told. An old lady, beautiful with "the spirit's youth
which never passes by," sits down by our side and tells us the story
of her life. She gives us an autobiography without calling it such,
and best of all, without apologizing for it. She points no moral;
she has too much delicacy for that. She speaks of the beauty of
her youth without vanity or false modesty as of any beautiful work
of her Creator. She deems the frank trustfulness of youth one of
life's least follies. She pours out with her recollections all the
sweetness and loveliness of a glorious soul, and with no thought
that she does so. The book has sentiment but no sentimentality.
There are humorous passages, pathetic passages and passages
exceeding sorrowful.

A writer of less talent, with those incidents and characters, would
have given us a sensation novel. But the book reveals its author to
be possessed of delicacy — a gift as rare as genius. She makes no
parade of grief, nor does she state it to be sacred, but she treats it
as if it were so. She does not prate of joy in high-flown phrase,
but speaks of it naturally, and in a sane manner as people whom we
meet every day do. The book is characterized by an absence of all
attempt at effect. It is not bookish. We have not read the story;
an old lady with a beautiful face told it to us. We have known her
and loved her, and now we reverence her memory. We revisit old
scenes and we think of what she told us of "A Walk in Childhood,"
and of the exquisite regret and tenderness with which she told it—
the mice in the nursery; the old nurse with her prophetic dreams;
the closet where the poor girl "Bell" hurried through her meals;
the bridge with its crowd of goody-venders, and the little deformed
child who sold night-caps; the barber; the "Claggum" shop; all
these are become as familiar as our own childhood.

Among the characters "Lissy" stands out starched and "prim,"
her reproofs and assertions knowing no verb but "ought," and
Buffy starts forth from his dark closet in his tight nankeen suit, and
we hear his thin voice moaning, "I wis' I was Mother Hubbard's
dog." We cannot doubt that the place for this book is among stand-
ard English novels. For humor, geniality, ease of diction, purity of
thought, delineation of character, though not perhaps for compre-
hensiveness, it deserves a high place. Yet this one book cannot
place the author, though the book itself be placed. We should
gladly welcome any further productions from the pen which has
written the "Queen of the County," giving us such vivid pictures
of English life sixty or seventy years ago, and giving them, too,
with such delicate touches of grace and beauty.   M.

MAINSTONE'S HOUSEKEEPER.

By Miss ELIZA METEYARD (SILVERPEN).

1 vol., 12mo. Elegant fancy cloth. Price $1.75.

———

Douglas Jerrold gave this distinguished English authoress this " *nom de plume*," and her style has the point, brightness, and delicacy which it suggests.— This is not a cook book as the title might mislead some to suppose, but a fresh, vigorous, powerful story of English country life, full of exquisite pictures of rural scenery, with a plot which is managed with great skill, and a surprise kept constantly ahead so that from the opening to the close the interest never flags. There is life in every page and a fresh, delicate, hearty sentiment pervades the book that exhilarates and charms indescribably.

The heroine — Charlotte the housekeeper — is one of the finest characters ever drawn, and merits unqualified commendation.

As a whole, for beauty of style and diction, passionate earnestness, effective contrasts, distinctness of plot, unity, and completeness, this novel is without a rival. It is a "midnight darling" that Charles Lamb would have exulted in, and perhaps the best as yet produced from a woman's pen.

SIMPLICITY AND FASCINATION.

BY ANNE BEALE.

1 *vol.*, 12*mo.*   *Elegant fancy cloth.*   *Price* $1.75.

———

It is not often that such a sound and yet readable English novel is republished in America.

The due mean between flashiness and dulness is hard to be attained, but we have it here.

There is neither a prosy page nor a sensational chapter in it.

It is a nice book for a clean hearth and an easy chair.

It is a natural, healthy book, written by a living person, about people of flesh and blood, who might have been our neighbors, and of events, which might happen to anybody. This is a great charm in a novel. This leaves a clean taste in the mouth, and a delicious memory of the feast.

The tone of it is high and true, without being obtrusively good. Such a book is as great a relief amid the sensational stories of the day, as a quiet little bit of " still life " is to the eye, after being blinded by the glaring colors of the French school.

This novel reproduces that exquisite tone or flavor so hard to express which permeates true English country life, and gives to it a peculiar charm unlike any other, which one having once seen and felt, lives as it were under a spell, and would never willingly allow to fade from their memory.

Too much cannot be said in praise of Simplicity and Fascination.

PIQUE:
A Tale of the English Aristocracy.

1 vol., 12mo. *Elegant fancy cloth.* *Price* $1.75.

———

Three thousand eight hundred and seventy-six new books were published in England this last year, which is about the average number of past years.

Thirteen years ago PIQUE was first published in London, and up to the present time, notwithstanding the enormous number of new books issued, the effect of which is to crowd the old ones out of sight, this remarkable novel has continued to have a large sale.

This is the strongest praise that can be bestowed on any book. It is not in the least "sensational," but relies solely on its rare beauty of style and truthfulness to nature for its popularity.

It has the merit of being amusing, pleasantly written, and engrossing.

The characters being high-bred men and women, are charming companions for an hour's solitude, and one puts the book aside regretfully, even as one closes the eyes on a delicious vision. The American edition has taken every one by surprise, that so remarkably good a novel should have so long escaped attention.

Every body is charmed with it, and its sale will continue for years to come.

FAITH GARTNEY'S GIRLHOOD,

By the Author of "The Gayworthys," "Boys at Chequasset"

1 vol., 12mo.   *Elegant fancy cloth.*   *Price* $ 1.75.

This charming story fills a void long felt for something for a young girl, growing into womanhood, to read.

It depicts that bewitching period in life, lying between FOURTEEN and TWENTY, with its noble aspirations, and fresh enthusiasms.   It is written by a very accomplished lady, and is "*the best book ever written for girls.*"

A lady of rare culture says, —

"'Faith Gartney's Girlhood,' is a noble, good work, that could only have been accomplished by an elevated mind united to a chaste, tender heart.   From the first page to the last, the impression is received of a life which has been lived; the characters are genuine, well drawn, skilfully presented; they are received at once with kind, friendly greeting, and followed with interest, till the last page compels a reluctant farewell.

"'The book is written for girls, growing as they grow to womanhood.' The story has an interest, far beyond that found in modern romances of the day, conveyed in pure, refined language; suggestive, pleasing thoughts are unfolded on every page; the reflective and descriptive passages are natural, simple, and exquisitely finished.

"In these days, when the tendency of society is to educate girls for heartless, aimless, factitious life, a book like this is to be welcomed and gratefully received.   Wherever it is read, it will be retained as a thoughtful, suggestive — if silent — friend."

A LOST LOVE.

BY ASHFORD OWEN.

1 vol., 12mo. Elegant fancy Cloth, with a Portrait of the Heroine
Price $1.25.

A few years ago a number of American novel readers got hold of a modest little English volume, entitled "A Lost Love," by Ashford Owen, and spread its reputation greatly in private companies by adjuring all their acquaintances to read it.

The book cannot fail to have a run, because it is thoroughly original in spirit, incident, sentiment, and character, and though the farthest in the world from being a "sensational" story, it will give the most *blase* novel reader a new sensation. It is a quietly intense representation of deep yet simple feeling and sentiment, in its development under unfavorable circumstances, and leaves on the heart a far finer ideal impression than most of the novels which do not equal it in reality and truth. We know nothing about the author, and it may be that his or her vein was exhausted in the production of a first book; but the vein itself, though it may be thin, is of pure gold.

☞ Read what the English Press says of it: —

The *London Athenæum*, says: "It is a story, full of grace and genius. We recommend our readers to get the book for themselves. No outline of the story would give any idea of its beauty."

The *Saturday Review*, says: "A striking, and original story: a work of genius and sensibility."

The *Westminster Review*, says: "A real picture of a woman's life; one who, while loving and thirsting to be loved, can give up her one hope in life, when sympathy and good sense demand the sacrifice."

The *Quarterly Review*, says: "A novel of great genius; beautiful and true as life itself."

The *Press*, says: "A tale at once moving and winning, natural and romantic, and certain to raise all the finer sympathies of the reader's nature. Its deep, pure sentiment, and admirable style, will win for it a lasting place in English fiction, as one of the truest and most touching pictures of woman's love."

THE GAYWORTHYS.

By the author of "FAITH GARTNEY'S GIRLHOOD," "BOYS AT CHEQUASSET." *

☞ American ladies and gentlemen travelling in England, are amazed and delighted to find "an American Novel" welcomed with such warmth and enthusiasm, by the "cultivated" and "influential," in all parts ot the Kingdom.

No American book since "Uncle Tom," is so universally known, read, and talked about.

The London journals, without exception, have given it a cordial welcome. Read what they say of it: —

"We wish to write our most appreciative word of this admirable and unexceptional book. We feel while we read it that a new master of fiction has arisen. . . . We can well afford to wait a few years now, if at the end we are to receive from the same pen a work of such a character and mark as "The Gayworthys." — *Eclectic Journal.*

"It is impossible not to welcome so genial a gift. Nothing so complete and delicately beautiful has come to England from America since Hawthorne's death, and there is more of America in 'The Gayworthys' than in 'The Scarlet Letter,' or 'The House with Seven Gables.' . . . We know not where so much tender feeling and wholesome thought are to be found together as in this history of the fortunes of the Gayworthys." — *Reader.*

"'The Gayworthys' comes to us very seasonably, for it belongs to a class of novels wanted more and more every day, yet daily growing scarcer. We have, therefore, a warmer welcome for the book before us as being a particularly favorable specimen of its class. Without the exciting strength of wine, it offers to feverish lips all the grateful coolness of the unfermented grape." — *Pall Mall Gazette.*

"We have no misgivings in promising our readers a rich treat in 'The Gayworthys.' . . . 'The Gayworthys' will become a great favorite." — *Nonconformist.*

" . . . The book is crowded with epigrams as incisive as this, yet incisive without malice or bitterness, cutting not so much from the sharpness of the thought as from its weight. There is deep kindliness in the following passage, as well as deep insight. . . . . The tone of the story, the curious sense of peace and kindliness which it produces, comes out well in that extract, and the reader quits it, feeling as he would have felt had he been gazing half an hour on that scene — with more confidence alike in nature and humanity, less care for the noisy rush of city life, and yet withal less fear of it. — *Spectator.*

"It is a pleasant book and will make for the producer friends." — *Saturday Review.*

"We venture to say no one who begins the book will leave it unfinished, or will deny that great additions have been made to his circle of acquaintance. He has been introduced to a New England village, and made acquainted with most of the leading villagers in a way which leaves the impression on him thenceforward that he knows them personally, that their fortunes and failures, and achievements, and misunderstandings are matters of interest to him, that he would like to know how Gershom Vose got on with his farm, and if Joanna Gair's marriage turned out happily, and if 'Say' Gair was as interesting as a farmer's wife as she has been as a little child."

TWICE LOST.

A NOVEL.

By S. M., Author of "LINNET'S TRIAL."

READ THE OPINIONS OF THE ENGLISH PRESS:

"Another first-rate novel by a woman! The plot well conceived and worked out, the characters individualized and clear-cut, and the story so admirably told that you are hurried along for two hours and a half with a smile often breaking out at the humor, a tear ready to start at the pathos, and with unflagging interest, till the heroine's release from all trouble is announced at the end. . . . We heartily recommend the book to all readers. It is more full of character than any book we remember since Charles Reade's 'Christie Johnstone.' "—*Reader.*

" 'Twice Lost' is an entertaining novel; the struggle between the high-spirited, generous, half-savage heroine, and her specious, handsome, unprincipled, soi-disant father, is exciting; and the sympathy of the reader is cleverly enlisted for the heroine, Lucia, from the first moment. The personages have all of them a certain look of reality, and there is a notion of likeness which insures the reader's interest. We can recommend ' Twice Lost' as a novel worth reading."—*Athenæum.*

"By far the cleverest book on our list is 'Twice Lost.' . . . This is bold and skilful drawing, and it is a fair sample of the earlier half of the volume. The combined vigor, ease, and perspicuity of the writing is unusual."— *Guardian.*

"Nothing can be better of its kind than the first portion of 'Twice Lost.' . . . The caustic humor and strong common sense which mark the sketches of character in this book, betray a keenness of observation and aptitude for producing a telling likeness with a few strokes, which need only a wider cultivation to secure a more complete success than has been attained in 'Twice Lost.' "
Westminster Review.

"It is quite clear that the author has given a good deal of thought to the construction of the story, with a view to producing strong interest without the use of the common sensational expedients. To say that 'Twice Lost' is very well written, and very interesting, would not be doing it justice.— *Morning Herald.*

"There can be no doubt of the author's power. She holds her characters and incidents well in hand, writes firmly, and often very happily, and there are many passages which indicate power much above mediocrity."— *London Review.*

"Not very often do we meet with a novel so thoroughly good as 'Twice Lost.' If, as may be assumed from both subject and style, its author is a woman, she may at once be classed with the Bronte sisters and George Eliot. She has the firm conception and distinct touch of the first-class artist. Her characters are real and individual. — *Press.*

"This is a well-written romantic tale, in which we find many pleasing incidents and some successful portraiture of character. The character of Miss Derwent, the companion and governess of the heroine, Miss Langley, is very well developed in the course of the narrative. The moral tone of the book is very good, and so far as religious matters are touched upon, they are treated with propriety and reverence."— *English Churchman.*

"The characters are well drawn—the situations are new, the sentiments are unsentimental, and the incidental remarks those of a clever woman who is reasonable and tolerant."— *Globe.*

"The plot of this tale is an original one, and well worked out. . . . We can sincerely recommend this tale; it is quite out of the general run of books, and is sure to prove an interesting one."— *Observer.*

"We notice this story because its authoress will one day, we believe, produce a powerful novel."— *Spectator.*

"The reader is carried along with unflagging and exciting interest, and the book is full of characters finely sketched, and of passages powerfully written."
— *Patriot.*

"That the author of 'Twice Lost' can write well, the book itself furnishes sufficient evidence."— *Nation.*

"This is a striking story. It has a freshness and originality about it which are very pleasant."— *Morning Advertiser.*

"Without being a sensation novel this is a most exciting and attractive story."
Daily News.

"A most romantic story, the interest being well sustained throughout, and every thing coming right at the end. Any one must be entertained by it.— *John Bull.*